THE HEART OF MARS

A Novel

ALSO BY CHUCK ROSENTHAL

THE HEART
OF MARS

A Novel

Chuck Rosenthal

 Hollyridge Press
Venice, California

Hollyridge Press
P.O. Box 2872
Venice, California 90294

Cover and Book Design by Rio Symth
Author Photo by Gary Goldstein
Cover Art:
"Endless Desert" by Paul Moore (Dreamstime.com)
Detail from "Horse" provided by Dreamstime.com (©Bertrand Collet)
Detail from "Horse Watching" by Natalia Sinjushina (Dreamstime.com)

Manufactured in the United States of America by Lightning Source

Publisher's Cataloging-In-Publication Data
(Prepared by The Donohue Group, Inc.)

Rosenthal, Chuck, 1951-
  The heart of Mars : a novel / Chuck Rosenthal.

    p. ; cm.

  ISBN-13: 978-0-9772298-5-7
  ISBN-10: 0-9772298-5-8

1. Mars (Planet)--Fiction. 2. Europa (Satellite)--Fiction. 3. Life on
other planets--Fiction. 4. Utopias--Fiction. 5. Science fiction. I. Title.

PS3568.O8368 H43 2006
813/.54   2006933186

16 15 14 13 12 11 10 09 08 07   10 9 8 7 6 5 4 3 2 1

To ,
xxxx
xxxx

The Heart of Mars

I

There has never been a good reason to be anywhere, let alone here. Yet here I am. And there you are. I am learning to write. And you, by now, must be learning how to read.

One of the big fish ferries from the ocean moon, the Gift Moon, Europa, had been hijacked and by all indications re-routed to the fourth planet, the desert planet, Mars. Where could you hide a billion fish on Mars? Who could keep them? Who could eat them? That's how my story begins. I was sent from Home, once called Earth, to investigate. There were robiots available, but you can't send a robiot to do a Nutian's work. In fact, you send a homan.

Long ago, one of the many things that was supposed to happen that didn't happen, was that things called machines would learn to think on their own. Non-biological space ships would travel at the speed of light. Or faster. But we have learned that there is an ebb and flow to everything. As the Nutian might say, we plumb run out of progress.

II

Coincidently, one of the many stories about Home before the Return of the Nutian has to do with Fish Wars. It was long before fish ferries and before the Nutian Return to save Home. I've found evidence that homan beings were organized under something called *government*, and government was a small group of people who told a larger group what to do. Usually the big group of people lived in about the same place, on a certain piece of geography, as their leaders, but not always. As you can imagine, it was good to be a governor, less good to be governed, so government created many misunderstandings.

Now during this time there was something called *writing*, which is what I am doing now. Well, actually not *right now* as you are reading. I made these symbols quite some time ago. But you are reading right now, just like you might listen to someone, or tactile-intuit them or smell them on bio-phone. I suppose you might know all of this already if you are, in fact, reading it, but for me this writing business is new, and though an ancient homan thing, a very unusual thing.

Once machines did the remembering for homans. It was called recording because machines didn't even know they had the messages. Can you imagine that?

III

Before the Return, homans spoke a thousand different languages and once wrote in them, too. Add to that the fact that we homans require two sexes to reproduce, quite an oddity in the known galaxy, and, well, you can imagine how difficult it was to agree on anything. Homanity was a species welded by conflict. Those ancient times were complex and brutal, yet in some ways beautiful, too. Do you know that idea? Beautiful? That's the thing. Writing has all these ancient homan ideas.

Cumbersome as it might seem, it seems that pages and pages of writing were once compiled in things called *books*. If you ever read a book before—and maybe you have and maybe you have not—but if you did, then you would know that it was hard to take very seriously everything that books said. They were very contradictory. And the books that said the craziest things were often the ones that people seemed to love the most. Sometimes governments believed in books and all the people under them were supposed to believe in that book as well.

It's hard to know when people gave up writing and began only speaking, but the Nutian say that it was at the point that homans started using machines to write. After a while, machines were doing all the writing. Almost all of the writing I have found in books has been done by machines. It is hard to know when the machines took over all the writing. Maybe some people still used their hands to write, as I am doing now, but it is very hard to produce many copies of what you have written without some help.

Once machines took over writing, some time in what homans then called the Twentieth Century, homans communicated almost exclusively through talking, though even in this, unless they were right in front of each other, they couldn't do it without machines. No wonder we have such a confusing view of our species as it existed before the

Return. Having multiple languages was confusing enough without getting machines which didn't know anything involved! Soon machines controlled almost all communication and, obviously, machines were not very independent thinkers.

IV

So, what is a machine? A machine was a non-biological system empowered by the immediate instigation of kenesis. It is a dead thing, a non-biological thing, that does things, but only when energy is injected into it, that is, they don't have their own energy. It is hard to imagine because we do not see them now and it is hard to know any of this for certain because all communication from these ancient times before the Return, at first writing, and then talking, too, was controlled by machines and it would seem that they perpetuated the most dreadful dreck upon the planet. Yet it came to pass that homans could not think, talk, or make a cup of coffee without them. Of course, there are no intuitile records, these systems being brought to us during the Return.

I read about the Fish Wars in a very unusual hand-written book, that is, a book handwritten by a homan being. It had a persons name on it, Charles Borromeo, and he called it his *journal.* Among other things, he called homans, *humans.* Apparently, near the end of the Age of Machines, the earth was filled with so many homan beings that some of them starved. And it seems there was much more land than there is now, too, before global warming and subsequent aqua-forming by the Nutian. *Nations* (not Nutian), that is people organized under governments, disagreed over fish. Some nations had many fish near their shores and not many people and some nations had many people in them but did not live near fish. Apparently some nations killed fish selfishly and indiscriminately. Because of all this people did an odd, though I have found thrilling, thing. Nations went to *war.* They got together with their machines and destroyed *each other* indiscriminately. Apparently this had happened many times before and not always over fish.

Well, anyway, I have somehow found my way back to fish and I suppose I am writing a very bad book. But besides fish, nations, it seems, if you can believe books, though the Nutian confirm it, fought over land, minerals, even books! If nations had very different favorite books, then their disagreements could be particularly vicious. I hope that someday people will kill each other over this book, though I somehow doubt it. And whether or not there are any *humans* anymore, *pure humans* anyway, if ever there were any, is a matter of debate. At this point, this is as much as I know.

V

I took a robiot ship to Gift Moon. You couldn't send a robiot alone to Gift Moon and you certainly couldn't send a Nutian. You can't trust a Nutian around fish, even the Nutian know that. The trip took a long time. It always took a long time and it still takes a long time. First Nutian, of course, simply go to sleep. They live for hundreds of years. Time means nothing to them and the more they sleep the older they live. I have not been so blessed. I have enough Nutian in me for tactile intuition, that is, I am somewhat intuitile, but I do not possess gills, nor do I grow my own water skin. Nonetheless, not even a First Nutian could survive long without protection in the seas of the Gift Moon, which are quite salty and cold.

Gift Moon is covered with a layer of ice. The ocean beneath is heated by the thermal dynamics of the moon's interior. The great mystery of Gift Moon Sea is the odd gap of misty, cold, breathable air between the sea and the ice, held there by an inexplicable force or tension and created, quite miraculously, by the exhalations of the sea itself. As you float upon the ocean on one of the great fish tankers, you gaze through the mist into the dazzling spectacle of broken light, as if the ice-sky above were a crystal mirror, the light of the dim, distant sun diffused into a mystical dance. Ambient, the fog twists into lambent figures so visceral that the wind currents, which hiss from the sky and gush from the water, moan inside these gesturing forms as flexing gusts ring them like ephemeral rags, luxuriant, plaintive, momentary. From these things that barely exist, and at that but for a moment, the air is filled with their murmuring: "why-why-why," and "iam-iam-iam-iam." I say this, as you will see, from experience, though it is said that the Nutian neither see nor hear them.

The sky melts in icy whimsy, in raindrops or sleet. It falls in rocks of hail or hangs in the sky as floating hills of powdery snow. Upon them and within them the figures slide, prance, roar, plead. Sometimes the sky lays down stalactites of ice, as if the sea were but a maze of icy bars around which the wailing figures dance and complain, while the ocean, like some beast, rises in geysers to press itself against the solid sky, sometimes breaking through and exploding upward, raging and bubbling to the frigid surface in immense columns which you can see as you circle the moon, as if the ocean itself were building castles of ice to beguile the living to the moon's frozen, dead surface. Sometimes, below, there is only the ocean and the wind and the slap and howl of weather on this moon where the weather itself is almost alive. And sometimes everything stops and it is deadly silent. Often there is so much death imitating life that it is hard to tell the difference.

Have I described this poorly? As I say, I am very new at this writing thing and it is hard to know what to put where and how to say it.

VI

My robiot swept the Gift Moon's surface, then hovered over the travel-navel, dropping its umbilical through the ice layer to the port of entry on the service dock. Umbilical travel from ship to surface is always intriguing, a lonely, slow slide of a mile or sometimes more through blackness and stars, an undulation, like birth, through the long, translucent cord of flesh; the sides of the chambers fluctuate with a hum, the soft music of cells murmur something earlier and more primal than your own life. And so, inevitably, you must land like a child out of the womb. Of course the trip is never so natal for the Nutian, who hatch into water from an egg, but for those of us more mammalian, Nutian travel is as a series of births, a passage from one biological chamber to another and there is a reverie to it that I suppose I shall someday miss.

There is not much on the Gift Moon to land on. Several islands, none of them as wide or long as a kilometer, push up through the ocean and serve as ports for the bioboats that bring the fish for transfer through the massive umbilical elevators to the fish freighters, giant bladders of salt water that hover in orbit above the ice. There is only one port for travelers, *The Port of Friends*, for the exclusive use of the Nutian. Of course, First Nutian have always believed that any self-conscious, biological entity is Nutian because all truly sentient things, by either evolution or creation, arose from amphibious life, and more so, all intelligent life forms have done so, most explicitly the First Nutian themselves who are amphibians, but other intelligent creatures as well, hominids and cetaceans (I suppose I need to add that neither fish nor reptiles have ever evolved to self-conscious intelligence) and marsupials like the Pets, one, or several of whom stood or sat in front of me, it was hard to tell, after I de-jelled from my landing.

As in most Nutian work colonies, the Pets ran the Gift Moon for the Nutian. Here, the Pets ran it and cetaceans worked it.

"Welcome," they said in homan. "You are Marl."

"Yes," I said. I then growled a formal greeting in Visceral Nutian, and ancient language used to communicate among or with non-intuitiles. Whether or not the Pets in front of me were intui-tactile, intui-tactile communication was far too intimate for a formal occasion like this and would be very impolitic between two creatures neither of whom were First Nutian. Besides, I had a respectful fear, if not revulsion, of Pets.

Pets themselves were olfactory communicators and when they first came in contact with us they found dogs much more intelligent than homans and assumed, on the basis of their olfactory complexity compared to ours, and by the way we fed and cared for canines, that dogs had run the planet before the Nutian Return. The creature in front of me seemed to explode, at first, with a flurry of noses, and emitted a penetrating odor akin to a frightened yak.

"There is no need," they said in homan, finally settling down upon themselves. "We are Elmoleonard."

"Elmoleonard," I said.

"Yes," they responded, "among others, and for lack of something more pronounceable."

I know I am writing horribly and so that is making you read horribly, but I must tell you here that Pets are more colony than character, more pack than person. Whatever their original or singular disposition, no one has ever seen it, for they are always in some group of furriness, clinging bodies, limbs and heads, which crawl about each other in constant, mutual affection, rubbing and petting themselves in total self-absorption and speaking, when they speak, by a kind of anarchy of mutual agreement, from one mouth or in unison. They often stink, as well. Aside from their furriness, Pets are seldom one kind of anything because they tend to colonize as easily as they reproduce and more than one homan, among other creatures, either by appropriation or by choice, has crawled into one of the pouches of a Pet and emerged months later as part of the furry, clinging hoard. Needless to say, Pets are quite huge.

It's said that Pets never learn anything, they just become things as things become them. This, of course, taken literally, is silly. But somewhere in my host there must have been something homan because something or someone in there spoke it.

"So, a homan this time," they said.

"This time?"

This response of mine, however innocuous, created quite a fury amidst the Pet and there was a great shuffling and puffing of fur, several mouths opening within and hissing "ktz" or "krtz." And then, "No. No ktz," until the hoard seemed to arrive at a unanimous "No krtz."

"I am aware of only a single incident that I am investigating," I told the creature or creatures. "The hi-jacked fish tanker."

There was yet more shuffling amid the fur across from me and I heard "moon," and "ghosts," whispered among them before I finally discerned, "Moon of Ghosts. This is the Moon of Ghosts."

"I'm aware," I told them. "I've studied the phenomena."

"You cannot have *studied* the phenomena," they said in almost a group sigh. They turned from me and moved forward in a kind of lumbering and rolling and hugging. Their smell had, for lack of a better description, become somewhat more diplomatic. "You must rest," they said. "And then we shall tell you what we know."

"Survive and contribute," I said to the Pet.

"Yes," they muttered. "Survive and contribute." But it was accompanied by an excremental odor.

VII

The accommodations were normal enough, if you'd traveled often, and I did. I had been a mediator between First Nutian and homan labor for some years, having visited the aqua-forming projects on the Rain Planet, Venus, the mobile jungle aquariums along the meridian of Mercury, and the many bio-mines among the atmospheres and on the volcanically active distant moons of the outer gas giants. I've seen the ruins of the ancient homan mineral mines on the asteroids, as well. Needless to say, by homan standards, I am quite old, over 180 Home years, this by the miracle of Nutian bio-genetics, and that was one of the beauties and benefits of having worked with them as I did. Most homans lived barely sixty years, much less if they lived in the Wild Zones of Home or on Mars, because the Nutian professed to prefer a policy of non-interference with other intelligent, biological species. My capacities for multiple forms of communication, as well as my skills in negotiation and investigation made me an exception. I am, as well, a descendant of some of the first Halfies, now extinct, the cross bred Nutian-homans who inhabited and aqua-formed Home at the beginning of the Return.

Assuming I might eventually find myself traveling to Mars, I'd spent a good deal of time studying the Martian Indigos. If it were not for their absolutely primitive living conditions, they would have been the first suspects in the fish-napping. They had expressed some discontent over plans to aqua-form the northern hemisphere of their planet, a project apparently begun some years ago using homan machine technology, a transformation which allowed the Indigos to migrate from Home, inhabit the Martian desert and scratch out the lives they lived today, if one could go so far as to call it living. They seemed to have little regard for the fact that despite having to relocate many northern tribes to the southern hemisphere, there was yet plenty of room for all of them, and aqua-forming the northern hemisphere would make the planet infinitely better for all life. In retrospect, this is precisely what they feared.

Oh, I feel I am getting nowhere fast. I have recently read an ancient homan book in which the author, writing about himself, wrote so slowly and poorly that he fell farther behind the task of recording his life every minute he wrote. Well, that's how I feel! And when I am not passing on misinformation, then I am babbling about things everybody already knows! I'm beginning to understand why homans stopped doing this!

In any regard, though a bio-room can feed you by osmosis—quite handy if you're hibernating—and though like most Nutian habitation, and technology as well, it quickly develops a soothing symbiosis with its occupant, homans, even homan-Nutian, like to eat. That is the worst part of travel. The Nutian are not much for cuisine. In fact they eat almost no vegetation, except medicinally, surviving solely on a diet of water life, predominantly fish, and even so, fresh water fish are preferred—raw—a delicacy which is hard to come by, at least in this solar system, except for in the few remaining fresh lakes and rivers of Home.

It had been a long time since I had actually eaten, so with not a little trepidation I sent a message through the Intuo to Elmoleonard, inquiring about food. They responded that they would be happy to share a meal with me and after a short rest I found my way to their quarters, a large enclosure more resembling a huge bed than a room, and smelling, as you might expect, quite like a zoo.

VIII

Elmoleonard in repose was not much different than Elmoleonard in formal regalia. They offered me kelp wine, both pale and syrupy, but strong, and several of them shared a drink with me. Given the sympathetic, if not symbiotic, nature of the species, on their own home world they had been exclusively vegetarian. Over time, with the incorporation of other species, along with whatever compromises they'd made to come to terms with the Nutian, like everyone else they ate fish, though cooked or marinated, for me a certain blessing. Nonetheless, Pets were noted for their exquisite gardens of flowering plants and vegetables.

We were served by a young cetacean of some kind, I guessed of bottle-nose dolphin descent. Unlike homans, cetaceans had survived, if barely, before the Return, as a number of species and I did not have a discerning eye for separating one from another except in the most general way. Despite having developed both primitive legs and hands, much like the Nutian themselves cetaceans were ill suited for prolonged terrestrial movement. On Home, homans filled these kinds of terrestrial, domestic positions, as well as work in space, where air-pressure suits were easier to maneuver in and maintain than water suits. Cetaceans generally worked in the water. But there were no homans here and it seemed that Elmoleonard preferred keeping a moist-room and tank in their quarters to divesting one of themselves from themselves, even briefly, to serve and cook.

The boy, who served steamed shellfish and sea weed, as well as krill broth, a cetacean delicacy, was a rather odorless being and one of the Pets communicated to him in clicks and whistles. After placing the food on low tables near us, he sat down, and a hand extended from Elmoleonard to pour the boy some wine. Elmoleonard relaxed visibly onto their pillows, several glasses of wine resting upon them in various furry niches, and emitted a smell reminiscent of a wet dog after rolling in a stagnant bog. Amid the constant stroking, murmurs of cooing, trilling and purring emerged from them, then quieted.

"So," they sighed harmoniously, "aren't we three something?"

I raised my kelp wine. "To health," I said. "Survive and contribute." I was there to gather information, not give it, and I did not wish to be baited.

Somewhere from the moving pile, in a voice almost homan, came a whisper. "An odd gathering of subjugated species." I heard it quite clearly. There was a flurry of motion after that, as if the creature were in search of the culprit. The cetacean looked away from me. The concept of subjugation did not exist in Nutian. It was an ancient, homan word, still used in the Wild Zones. Since the Return, each species had found its place on Home, operating freely within its biological destiny for the perpetuation of living things which possessed the capacity for thought or emotion or both. The use of a pre-Return word which suggested dissatisfaction might be considered treason had the Nutian a concept of treason.

"If I were here to do more than simply gather information, would that not make you a suspect?" I said to the Pet.

The air was suddenly charged with tension, as well as a rather odiferous, sweet emission. The creature gathered itself, returning to its altogether voice, like a choir. "Were we a possible suspect, would we dare say something suspicious?"

As I have said, I was not well experienced in dealing with Pets. They were not from our system and I encountered them rarely on Home where they most often served as liaisons in the Wild Zones, high altitude islands, dry, cold and uncomfortable to the Nutian, where homan separatists lived free of Nutian culture.

"Your logic could lead me just as easily to the opposite… conjecture," I said, not wishing to intimate that I was interested, this early in my investigation, to arrive at any conclusions. I offered a casual chuckle, though I was not sure how the Pets responded to laughter. I turned to the cetacean boy. "The soup is delicious," I said.

He nodded and said, "Thank you," in that high whine character-istic of porpoises when they spoke homan, song-like, almost dreamy. Clearly feeling more comfortable, he moved closer to my host who extended a heavy paw and pulled him to his side. From both the ceta-cean and the Pet a soft "eee-eee" emerged as the dolphin boy nuzzled into the Pet's fur.

"We have tried hard to convince him to join us," said a voice deep in the center of my host, "but he is very different and we do not know if it has ever been done. He needs water so badly, the transformation might be impossible."

The appetizers had sated my hunger and the kelp wine, if not complex, filled me with seductive relaxation. A thin, furry arm and hand unfolded from the Pet and reached out to me, the smell on its fingertips like the odor of a woman making love, when the jewel of her perspiration mixes with her perfumes, moist, familiar, intimate. I was shocked and cannot deny that I felt inexplicable arousal and longing. When I reached out and touched the hand, the glazing of our finger-tips felt like a kiss, but not a kiss of seduction but the soothing, tactile murmur of two lovers already sated. When I did not come forward the hand withdrew like a question mark, slowly and sadly falling into crea-tures in front of me.

"You must be very loyal," they said. "For them to send you."

"Are we not all loyal?" I said, but immediately, idiotically, felt as if that loyalty somehow betrayed a deeper trust already bonded with the being before me. It is that moment, if you have been on these kinds of missions, and encountered these kinds of situations, both new and alien, when your purpose, your values, seem suddenly to have been pulled out from under you, and you inflate with fear, you float in fear, feeling powerless and immobilized. Though I had learned to wait. To wait out the fear. To relax and pay attention. "When you said I was the first homan," I said cautiously, "you implied that others, Nutian, I would have to surmise, have preceded me, and from that I can induce that there would have been reasons for them to come, reasons I have not been told, reasons, I must suppose, I was expected to discover, or never discover."

The multitude in front of me appeared to relax under my caution. They emitted a general boil of murmuring and self-affection and the odor of a camel drinking water under the sun, a kind of satisfied, exhausted smell, yet one filled as much with anticipation as pleasure. Already, in this brief time, despite my limited olfactory capacities, I had come to feel the subtleties of this odiferous syntax. "Let us—let us—let us," they said in a chorus reminiscent of *Row, Row, Row Your Boat*, a jingle still sung to children on Home. "What do you know of us?" someone finally said.

I poured myself more wine, and poured for them, too, as well as the boy. And then I told Elmoleonard what I knew.

IX

What everyone knew. Like Home, their planet had been seeded with life by the Nutian, and like Home, as well, life there evolved from amphibians. For a very long time, the Dry Time the Nutian called it, there was a collapse of Nutian technology. Among other things, they lost intra-galactic travel. In that time, planets like the Pet world, and Home, evolved on their own.

"Yes," whispered someone from inside my host, "it seems to have been quite a long time."

"Eons, it seems, of course," I said.

When inter-system travel was renewed, I continued, the Nutian returned and watched us for a long time. I assumed that's the way it was for the Pets, too. But we went into decline on Home. We had, as the Nutian say, run out of progress. Homan technology had run amuck, global warming began, oceans levels rose and cataclysmic storms ravaged the planet; there were massive extinctions across species and a near annihilation of the food chain; homan population declined from twelve billion to less than two; within time a new ice age was likely to terminate almost all sentient forms on the planet for millions of years. That's when the Nutian stepped in. That was the Return. They stabilized the planet, replaced machines with superior, bio-technology, and allowed things to develop again under their benevolent anarchism. Everything I knew about the Pet home world reiterated, more or less, what had happened on Home.

Of them and their world, I told them what almost everyone knew. They were a symbiotic species, or group of species, very old. They communicated by smell. Their solar system was older than ours and geological activity had ceased on their world. This led to a gradual, planet-wide degeneration of their ecosystem. Because the planet had been geologically dormant for an eon, there was little variation of terrestrial altitude and when the oceans rose the planet was left as either sea or swamp. Most of the Pets perished before the Nutian could stabilize the eco-system.

"Yes," said a voice from deep within Elmoleonard, "it seems they stepped in a bit late."

X

The being stirred with movement again. They were glorious to watch, a rainbow of fur and motion. Some of the creatures within looked as small as my hand and still others as large as me or larger. An odor arose like the smell of freshly turned earth. The cetacean boy, a bit dry and gasping, excused himself, I assumed to return to his wet room and tank.

Elmoleonard's subtlety and complexity went beyond physical multiplicity. Sensing both my uneasiness over their potential questioning of Nutian motives, as well as the resultant contradiction of their keeping the boy, the Pet lifted a hand. "Consider the alternatives, Marl," they whispered.

"I'm not fully acquainted with the alternatives," I said.

"You shall be," one of them chimed.

Some shushing arose from Elmoleonard and then a singular voice, the softest, deepest one, began speaking. It is hard to remember precisely, but they told me that they had long been a culture that eschewed technology. For them, it added nothing to life. And it had taken centuries upon centuries for the sentient forms on their planet to become so mutually sympathetic. Of course, not all were. Carnivores, in particular, were resistant to appropriation, though the Pets loved them and they proved particularly advantageous when the Pets had to adapt to eating fish. Large herd animals were now difficult to accommodate, though on the Pet home world some large colonies once lived on the backs of one or more herding beasts.

"That would have been marvelous to see," I said to Elmoleonard.

"Better yet, to smell," they replied.

Each Pet had a marsupial parent-mother who served as the core sentience around which the furry anarchy gathered itself and by means of which the colony reproduced. Any member of the colony could procreate with the parent-mother, a process which could best be described as a shedding of the biological self inside the parent's pouch. It took a long time, years, and it involved the absorption or extinction of the original seed animal in the creation of the offspring, a synthesis of the parent-mother and the seed. This was procreation, quite a different thing entirely from the appropriation of a new individual from outside the Pet itself, though an appropriated species became capable of pro-creating after transformation. Of course, the Pets' almost universal affection for other beings brought in genetic strains which prevented in-breeding. And the constant mixing and appropriation of species brought to the sentience of the planet a shared quotient of sympathy and intelligence. On the Pet home world, most animals were pretty smart.

Individual Pet colonies changed and evolved rather quickly. And it was difficult to know when a given colony had, in fact, passed away. In fact, it was impossible. Single Pet colonies traced their existence to the beginning of memory. Yet if individual members of the colony lived almost eternally, by means of sacrificing their individuality through creative absorption, the marsupial parent-mothers, though mutually perpetuated by the acts of both appropriation and procrea-tion, did eventually die, and it was an absolute necessity for the colony to create a new parent-mother to maintain the integrity of the entity before the death of the central parent. This was an act of singular con-centration and biological control on the part of the aging parent-mother, because the heir had to be marsupial enough and similar enough to assume parenthood of the colony. Not that colonies them-selves could not merge. On their home world some colonies grew quite large for a time, but these proved unmanageable, difficult to move and feed, and less intimate.

"Can any of you leave yourself?" I asked. "Migrate?"

"Why would anyone do that?" chimed a choir of voices. For the first time I detected a murmur of giggling as the being in front of me erupted into sort of pulsing and thumping. Finally, the soft, almost fe-male voice I'd heard earlier whispered, "Yes. Yes."

"And your home, it was not called Pet," I said to Elmoleonard then.

"No," they said, and emitted an odor of overwhelming euphoria and power. I had never felt more security and peace than I did while swimming in that odor, though there was nostalgia there, and longing, and a sympathy more transcendent than anything a homan might call love. I understood quite simply that they called it *Paradise*.

XI

I had learned, in my brief time with Elmoleonard, to watch them, smell them, listen to them the way a man watches a moon through the fog. For to them the meaning of a story was not inside, but outside, enveloping the tale which brought it out only as a glow brought out a haze, in the likeness of one of those misty halos that sometimes are made visible by the spectral illumination of moonshine. I suppose, better, that their conversation was not much different than themselves, and one needed to pick out the essence from the swarm, an essence which was always moving and seldom in the center.

"It is nothing," they whispered. "We were thinking of the time when the Nutian first came."

You might think this just another example of how my writing, and maybe all writing, is so senseless and meandering, but I admit that I am at fault. Please do not condemn the form for my clumsiness. Not yet. Like you, I had to wonder about why I had been told all that I had been told. And why I had been asked what I had been asked. I concluded that the morale of the tale was that Pets had very long memories, and that those memories might contradict something that I had said. But what of it? First Nutian were without laws, without possessions, without discord, without philosophy. If we other species were more perturbable, we would yet find our own place among them in our own way. We were all Nutian now. In all the solar system, the sun never stopped warming some planet, some ocean, some moon that was not Nuition. Whatever you might think, the facts are in front of you and you live.

I sat quietly before my host, contemplating. The cetacean boy, replenished and moist, arrived with an exquisitely poached ocean salmon, battered and fried cod, and marinated sea perch along with a warm salad of several vegetables I did not recognize, the smell of which was indescribably complex. This arrived on huge platters as, in legend, homans called Argentines once served the flesh of steers. Of course, on Home, we no longer ate the flesh of intelligent life, except possibly in the Wild Zones. I don't know. And I had not noticed at first the delicacy with which the Pets took their food, as if it were less eating than olfactory communion. The cetacean brought another bottle of kelp wine.

I ate till I was full. After days of space travel it felt good to be with another being, or beings, feel real food in my stomach, real inebriation coat my brain. The Pet, Elmoleonard, began to roll upon itself and preen, an odd mixture of sophistication and primitive sensuality. The cetacean brought out fresh glasses shaped like bulbs and poured a sweet elixir, almost deadly. My head spun the moment the fumes touched my nostrils.

"You said there were others before me," I finally said again, as if there were nothing left for me to do but be direct.

"Nutians," said the Pet.

"What happened?"

"There is unrest, Marl."

"Unrest?"

"Yes," they said. "Here."

"Tomorrow," I said, my head tilting inside itself, trying to find one place quiet and clear. "I'll visit a fishing ship."

"But there is unrest. There are the ghosts. And pirates. There is some danger."

"Pirates!" I laughed. "Pirates are a pre-historical, homan myth." Suddenly my head began to clear. The cetacean boy was helping me to my feet.

"Yes," said the choir of my host. "Tomorrow."

I awoke in the dark, from a slumber filled with ice and mist, my teeth chattering with cold. I remembered. The ocean moon. I was on the ocean moon, the Gift Moon, the Moon of Ghosts. And as I shivered I felt that longing that one gets for home, for something ancient and deep like a raging fire, a loved one, a glass of red wine, something homan, something. Space sickness, I told myself. Travel sickness. Then

I saw the figure not five meters from my bed. At first I thought it mist, but then I made out the body of a homan female, quiet, absolutely motionless. She was covered with a light, furry down, gray with black like an appaloosa horse, yet golden hair poured from her head and over her neck, her slender shoulders, her full breasts. My head ached, yet as I shivered in the wet cold, I distinctively smelled my name in the air.

"Why am I so cold?"

"Let me warm you," she said, coming to my bed. She moved upon me like a warm breath, a bath, a gentle sweat. In an instant I had never felt such pleasure, nor longing. Nor did I realize until then, in our communion which lasted through the bitter cold night, that my life, my heart, had until that moment been filled with darkness and solitude.

XII

The ocean of the Gift Moon is always dipped in dim light as the ceiling of ice refracts the constant reflection of the bright gas giant Jupiter or the direct light of the distant sun. A dim world pinned between dim light, it is never day and never night, and forever both dawn and dusk. Like most places you travel when you leave Home, time loses itself inside itself in perennial constancy.

Bio-rooms seek the rhythms of their guests and after some time mine, now nurturing two of us, found itself around us and began to bring a warm luminescent glow to its walls, a light much like the incandescent micro-fauna in the oceans of Home. I awoke in the arms of my companion, urged helplessly by my own instinct to caress as incessantly as I received her caresses.

"So," I said to her softly, staring into her round, dazzling eyes, one *azul* and the other golden. "Are you Elmo or Leonard?"

"I am neither and neither are they," she said, looking away. She was simply and absolutely erotic and emitted a gorgeous, complex odor, indescribable but that it went directly from my nose to my groin, and just as well, for I found her almost incapable of communication if we were not genitally embedded and entwined; then, in rhythmic embrace, my heart on edge and my breath laboring just beyond my desire to converse, my chest and thighs surging on the edge of orgasm, she relaxed, her hands moving over me, her soft down softer than her seductive softness. "I am L."

"The first L or the second L?" I panted.

"Both," she laughed.

I clutched her shoulders, gripped her face as she pinned her small ears. Her eyes rolled in her head and then fixed on mine. If there was any pleasure greater and more incalculable than mine, it was that of watching hers.

"You separated," I whispered.

"We like you."

I had been in love. I am homan and have been in love. Had passionate affairs, long marriages, born children who I watched live and die, and never had I known more passion than in that instant or that of the night before. And I am not a young man. Not youthful. In fact solidly middle-aged, if well-preserved. But I had never known this kind of raging pleasure. Never known it before. There, in that ecstasy, she smelled my name to me, and hers, and I learned that she had met El-moleonard in the Wild Zone of the mountains on the northwest fringe of Home's central land mass. She said a word, a name, that I did not recognize. *Alps.* She had once been homan and wore an amulet around her neck, held by a string of hide, an amulet with a creature I didn't recognize, a kind of lizard with fire blazing from its throat.

XIII

All questions one might have about the Pets fall way in their embrace. Language and logic become superfluous if not impossible. Beyond the tactile and the olfactory, there is simply nothing left for consciousness to do. There is nothing it can do. Science and technology are irrelevant. The miracle of their existence is that they have stayed alive at all; with pleasure so full, so insular, when would you eat? Yet in time, some timeless stretch of time, I fell into a rhythm of addiction and found I could hold, for moments, a barren thought and, indeed, this would seem the discipline of being a Pet and surviving. Yet now, even the bio-room itself seemed to yearn for us and the air and walls around us sighed with longing.

XIV

At some point I came, but soon aroused and came again and yet again, really quite beyond my abilities, until I could do it no more. L moved around me. She seemed everywhere around me. Remembering my mission, I fell into horrid satisfaction, exhaustion and despair. In this breech, briefly, I spoke to her in smells and words, an irreproducible dialogue which I account for here but vaguely.

"I had forgotten," she said, "what it was like to be homan."

"That was not homan," I told her.

And then she offered her laugh, the most amazing, distinctive trill and giggle. But I learned that Elmoleonard had once administered her Wild Zone and that is when she appropriated. Homan life in the zones was short and brutal. She had been born there and saw no hope.

"Why not live among the Nutian?"

"They're too dutiful," she said. "And joyless."

Though at the time I did not understand the second term, it's root being *joy*, an ancient word. "We are all Nutian," I said, for without the Return there would have been no humanity at all. We were a species ripped apart by our own individuality whose machine technology was but an instrument of our greed. The planet had been on the verge of destruction. If not for the Return, all life would have been as in the Wild Zones. "No," she said. "No." She got up from the bed, her form lithe and full, cat-like, and her departure filled me with vacuous longing.

"Don't leave," I said.

"Join us."

"Why did you come?"

"Join us."

"I cannot."

"Join," she said. "Join." Though she did not say it, really, but emitted an odor which filled the space around me with bliss. When she left, the room itself pulsed and ached for her return.

XV

We traveled to the fishing fleet by submarine. I regained my composure and dressed in the water-leathers I'd brought with me on my flight. Elmoleonard moved cumbersomely aboard our vessel, a wide, long ship shaped like a whale-shark. As I have said, the Nutian were never in a hurry, even during space travel, and our submarine swam, more or less, around the stable cabin where Elmoleonard and I bided our journey, its head and tail sloughing slowly and rhythmically through the depths of the cold, green sea.

Nutian bio-technology is methodical, and efficient in that sense, if one is committed to neither simplicity nor speed. For the Nutian, the simplest theory or model, the most direct plan, the most efficient technology, is not always conceived as the best, and often the most basic reduction requires more explanation than a simple, intuitive response. Everything finds its own way, even in travel and communication, so there was no precise way of knowing where the fishing fleets were at that time, nor any way of directly communicating with them. As our ship swam, almost directionless, beneath the sea, it let out an eerie series of cries and songs and waited to hear the song of the nearest fleet returned, from which it would eventually gather its direction.

Even the Nutians themselves, who have tremendous intuitive powers, communicate over distances less by device than assertive intentionality, though one doesn't so much as send a message as influence a response through, for lack of a better term, a kind of harmonic resonance. Compared to talking it might seem rather vague, but, in fact, it precludes argument, a bane of homan communication. Needless to say, Nutian do not disagree among each other very much, nor are they easily persuaded or dissuaded, so as a species, in their lethargic way, they get a lot done. And the mood among them is so thoroughly communal, so utterly filled with the sense of *we*, concepts of greed or generosity are irrelevant. This was the sense of tedious duty to which L had referred, duty being, I suppose, as close as a homan could come to it.

I know I am once again writing in my horrible way (though I am hoping that you are inexperienced enough at reading to think that this is how it is done—a small joke—in fact I hope that you are simply eager and forgiving and not too bored), but I have wandered in this way, much as a Nutian submarine, to explain—in the case that when you read this, things have changed drastically since now, and more explicit and direct forms of communication, as in the days of ancient homanity, have returned—why I had such little communication with the Nutians themselves on Home.

In the meantime, in fact a much longer time than it probably took you to read the last digression, we were still wandering through the cold ocean of Gift Moon as Elmoleonard, now almost oblivious to my presence, rolled and soothed themselves in a soft corner of the ship, and I gazed upon them, searching and listening and smelling for L amid the furry lathering. Had I known what I know now, having read some of the confusing detective histories written by ancient homan machines—yet still not knowing how much to trust them—I would have been more suspicious of L's visitation, though I was then suspicious enough, which went against all of my Nutian training. Nutians hide little, if they have little to hide. Likely, quite simply, L missed being homan, as she said. And now I missed her. That was the rub. Now I missed her. And under the cascade of Elmoleonard's equivocality about Nutian dominion during our first meeting, I began to suspect her as an emissary, if not more, or worse, a spy. Suddenly I was fearful and felt at the disadvantage of my affection, as well as ambivalent and uncertain about Elmoleonard himself, my ambassador and guide. What's more, it would seem I was jealous of them and their rampant affection to which I was hideously drawn.

The creature in front of me rose up slightly and extended several noses. "You don't smell so good, Marl," they said.

"You mean *well*," I told them. "You mean I do poorly at smelling."

"No, you smell bad," they intoned. "You stink of odd emotions."

It was then that our ship shuddered amid wails and moans, then responded with a sort of gleeful skreeing of its own.

"We have located them," Elmoleonard said. They stood, or at least got bigger, and shuffled toward the aft where there was an air sphere and lift. As I've said, you might find this world of ice and water completely unfit for the Pets if they were not so famed as administrators and diplomats. On the surface, Elmoleonard would occupy a large, pliable bubble which kept them dry and warm, and yet let air filter through its flexible walls.

They stopped and shifted around themselves before entering the aft chamber, apparently facing me again. "You will need to be clear-headed," they said to me in an odiferous gust. "It could be quite a shock, Marl."

"I have seen most of this solar system," I said to them.

"And why not this, Marl? Why are you the first homan?"

"Is that rhetorical?"

There arose a shuffling among the Pet, and then that kind of echoing chorus of repeating voices, as if they were coming to agreement with themselves on the spot, one after another. "The ghosts are real," someone whispered, and then again and again from throughout the shuffling fur. "The ghosts are real. The ghosts are real." There followed an odor of frightful repugnance, transparent and icy.

I braced myself against it. "I do not doubt I shall see them," I said.

"They are sentient, Marl."

"They are momentary," I said. "Wisps of mist."

"What is a moment? What is a moment? What is a moment?" echoed my host.

"What is the point?" I finally said.

"They might seem familiar to you."

"Familiar?"

"Marl, they are ghosts."

XVI

Our ship now began to push through the water with urgency, its fins spreading and pushing at its sides, the light brightening through its translucent walls as we began to surface.

"Do you see them?" I asked.

"We do."

"Are they harmful?" I said.

"It depends on how you can be harmed. You must keep your composure."

"I am very capable," I said.

A hand reached out from Elmoleonard and touched my shoulder and I recognized it as L's. I felt a rush of euphoria and desire and a sweet, edgeless odor like fresh roses. "We care for you, Marl," they said, though this time I felt certain that I heard L's silken voice trill from deep amid the beast. The hand ran down my arm. A finger lightly touched my palm. "There is more."

"Yes?"

"There are the pirates."

"Pirates do not make sense!" I said to them. "There is plenty of everything! Everything is shared!"

"You might find differently, Marl. If the pirates come, you should know they are carnivorous. They do not steal, they destroy. They eat. They eat everything."

"Flesh?"

"Everything. They are of the Cetacean species Orc."

"There are no Orcas on Gift Moon."

"Marl, you say there are no ghosts. You say there are no Orcas. We live here, Marl."

"Could they have hijacked the fish ship?" I asked.

"They eat everything."

"The Nutian emissaries," I said.

"Yes," said Elmoleonard.

Both of L's hands were upon my shoulders now, massaging my neck, my back. "But not you," I said.

"We did not come here with the Nutian," said the Pet.

I stood quietly with the Pet as the ship sang and swam not fifty meters from the surface now, the light dim yet dazzling above, dancing from the ice floes and mist and into the emerald sea. L took her hands from me and I waited as Elmoleonard completed their submersion into the bubble, then I joined them aft on the lift.

"Soon?" I said to them.

"Count your breaths," they said, which was an old Nutian saying for waiting. It was then that I heard L's remarkable, soft laugh from within the mound of roving bodies and fur. For the Nutian, waiting is. For other species it can be more difficult.

XVII

I waited. I waited in the emerald sea, in the suspended ship, in the suspended light; in the ocean of the Gift Moon, once Europa, waited in the aft of a swimming ship under the pounding of its swinging tail, in a singing ship under the pounding of its lumpy song, its moans; the whistles and whaas of the Cetacean fleet blooming above us, around us, as if we were suspended in a sob, a sigh, an ocean, a sea, a moon of moaning, of sad sympathy, of pity. I felt like the buried dead waiting to emerge into the air of the dead, the breath of the dead, the lives of the dead, the dead more alive than anything living; a man without a pulse waiting to emerge into a beating heart.

I apologize. I am a bad writer. How these words fail.

XVIII

Then the ship rose from the sea into the glacial radiance, the lift pushing us silently into the cavernous surface of the moon, onto the impossible sea turbulent with the backs of whales. Soon I could make out that we were not in the open sea at all but in the center of a tank a kilometer long and at least as wide, and in the distance another and another and another. Icebergs rose like castles, twisting into cones and spires, growing as I watched, stretching toward the crystal sky as others groaned and collapsed, the sea roaring under them.

If the ocean and ice were not enough enraged, then the surface of the sea was almost maniacal. My ears hurt from the screams of the whales. Beyond the nets, a circle of huge grays surrounded a school of lunging tuna, herding the baffled fish toward our tank. The fish surged, jumped, plunged, but around the circle, and beneath, other rings of whales drove them in. Here were these great baleened beasts, hunting what they could not even eat, a miracle of Nutian persuasion, as I noted to Elmoleonard.

"An old skill, honed a million years before there were homans, or *humans*," they said. Despite my exhilaration and the madness of activity around us, the Pet seemed paradoxically morose.

"Possibly taught to them by the original Nutian," I suggested, but received only silence.

Our ship slowly wagged its way to a platform near the end of the tank where there was an interior, as well as the workings for an umbilical elevator. Outside the structure another huge Pet sat stroking itself inside a bubble like Elmoleonard's. They called themselves Ermanmelville and had spent some time on Home in the Appalachian Isles, a forested, Wild Zone archipelago in the northeast sea of what was once something called North America. They sat in front of an intui-panel that they called a skreeboard, which ran a gamut of sonar dialects that could communicate with the different cetaceans.

Ermanmelville no longer spoke any homan idioms, but explained to me through Elmoleonard that the larger cetaceans, fins, blues, and hump backs, who had longer ranges and preferred roaming more than the migratory grays, ran the edges of the fleet in hunting parties and herded the fish in the general direction of the gray whales who sprang the final trap on the fish just outside the tank, in the capture field, pushing the schools through the one-way membrane nets of the tank. The inside of the tank was worked by various species of dolphins, the only toothed members of the order I saw working the fleet. These creatures had been altered, like Elmoleonard's cetacean boy, some more radically than others, and swam through the tank with short, finned arms and legs, much like fish people. They were capable of manipulating the biotechnology: the nets, the phlegm walls, the underground components of the elevator. The umbilical transport on this ship, most of which, of course, was under water, moved the fish to the flagship where the space-umbilical transferred the catch, live, to the fish freighter in stationary orbit above the moon.

"Why not use pinipeds for this?" I said.

"They're mischievous and need land to procreate," said Elmoleonard. "And they can be appropriated by us."

"Pets run the freighters," I said.

"Yes," Ermanmelville responded, and released a scent which was rather odious.

I spent some hours watching the process before requesting a skiff to take me into the tank. "They won't hurt me," I said, though I meant it as much an inquiry as anything.

Elmoleonard released a tentative, yet benevolent odor, like the boiling of an herb tea.

"So it is not likely," I said and had the skiff brought to the dock where I embarked myself into the squirreling sea. Over the hood of my water-leathers I wore goggles which were composed of a clear, self-cleaning membrane that could both magnify and telescope my eyesight. They were equipped, as well, with an intuo-cell in resonance with Ermanmelville's skreeboard, which allowed me to communicate with the dolphins as quickly and primitively as I could translate.

My first moments aboard the skiff were the most remarkable moments of my life, if not for the fact that they were exceeded by each moment that was to follow. From the water level the ocean rose and fell in mountainous, green waves beneath the silver sky. Castles of ice formed and fell, frozen columns rained from above, stood for moments gigantically, then collapsed. Yet other formations seemed to hold together like cities of ice and when I was not careful I found myself wandering within them, remembering lives I never knew. Beneath me now, the black backs of the cetaceans surged. Some of them raised their heads, crying with curiosity, "What? What? What are you?"

"Nutian, like you," I whistled. "And Homan."

The sea beneath me bristled as the creatures broke the surface around me and the air sizzled with dolphin howls which I translated as *Landhoman*. "We are Homan. We are from Home, too," they said.

"You aren't from the sea of the Gift Moon?"

"Born here, but Homan," said one. "Are you also a slave?"

At the time I had seldom heard the word *slave*, knowing it only as Wild Zone slang for we Homan-Nutian outside the Zones. As for the cetaceans, there were few, if any, alive in the oceans of Home itself. Driven to near extinction before the Return, almost all of the living species now survived here on Gift Moon, saved by Nutian intervention. As to why the cetaceans were not rejuvenated on Home there were dozens of reasons, most significantly that the biosphere had been irrevocably altered during the Age of Machines. Though replenished by Nutian bio-technology, early emergency measures centered on stabilizing the global greenhouse gasses in order to prevent a consequential ice age, not on making Home oceans habitable for whales. Home was now stabilized as a planet of 90% low-salinated oceans and wetlands. However well the remaining Homans could adapt, the cetaceans could not, and the Nutian released them here on Gift Moon where they would do best, to survive and contribute, as we all did.

"I am like you," I said to the dolphin. It was difficult to conceive how creatures like these would have anything to do with hijacking a space freighter to a desert planet, but as a Nutian I understood that all things were interconnected. Fish were hijacked and here there were the fish. "Are there pod leaders here?" I asked.

But suddenly, as if the ocean had paused to inhale, the sea fell flat and silent. The horizon cleared of columns and castles, the backs of the cetaceans disappeared beneath water's surface. It was as if the moon were dead and I stood in my skiff on a flat, dead, green calm expanse. I glanced to the dock where the Pets turned in furry unison toward the line where the frozen silver sky met the silent green sea. There, on the edge of sight, a white fog sat, no, advanced, and then began to swirl as if filled with the misty bodies of a hundred thousand beings. A slight wind stirred, but it was as much sound as wind, and faintly, ever so faintly on the edge of hearing, I discerned what I thought to be a tune. It was nothing that I had ever heard before, yet was both haunting and rhythmic, as if the air itself were marching in the distance.

XIX

The fog advanced and the sound-wind grew louder as the whole of Ermanmelville now motioned frantically for me to return my skiff. Yet I was too confounded to make my intentions clear and the little boat trembled beneath me in mimicry of my own trembling. Now the cloud advanced like a wall of swarming ghosts and the wind whistled with its song. Below me in the water the dolphins rose to that visceral fog, their cries in a high, screaming rhythm as if squeals were somehow drums. As the fog rolled toward the tank I began to make out the figures inside, which were themselves dolphins; the air around me filling with white, misty dolphins, swimming, dissipating, forming again only to again disappear, the dolphins beneath me in the turbulent sea whistling the dirge from which I could now make out a few words—*work and work, labor and death, work and labor and death*—there was a dance of this above me in the air and in the sea below and in the wild, whistling rhythmic song, somewhere between breath and whistle, phantom and fog.

I gathered my wits and my boat and guided it to the dock, embarking. There the Pets swarmed upon themselves in a frenzy.

"What is it?" I said.

"To whom?" said Elmoleonard.

Even as we spoke the ocean heaved beneath us, an island of ice rising to our right as the sky fell to meet it. There, before me, formed a city from my memory, and in it, behind the windows of homes and shops, within the vehicles lingering in its streets, shadowy faces, wisps of life appeared, faded, and appeared again. The inhabitants floated from home to home, to theater and shop, on frail boats between frail palaces, so shimmering and pale it was as if they were reflections of mirages, mirrors of mirrors.

Now, above the din of the cetacean work song, came whispers deeper than memory, my mother's voice, a lullaby, my father humming as he worked.

"Do you see them?" I said to the Pets.

"We see an island," Elmoleonard said. "Verdant. Swarming with life and sympathy."

I spoke to Ermanmelville. "You have seen this before," I said.

"Yes," they affirmed, releasing a cautious, steady odor, like roasting nuts.

"What could they be?"

"The ghosts."

"Yet there is an island of ice," I said.

And upon the island now the twisting forms began to writhe and dance, appearing, disappearing, slipping from light posts to alley ways at the edge of my sight. When I looked straight on I saw nothing, ice, air, sea, but on the edge of my sight danced a thousand momentary figures, beings, all of them familiar and old and yet unnamable, their voices, their eerie song in the air around me as furtive as thought, in fact now dancing in cadence inside me.

"*Why-why-why?*" they whispered.

"I do not know."

"*We are-we are.*"

"You are not."

"*Why-why?*"

"Marl," I heard. Elmoleonard. "You mustn't go to them Marl. They are not like us."

I looked out upon the sea of ghosts, the isle of ice and ghosts, the moon of ghosts.

What were they? Where were they?

"*Yes-yes-yes,*" I heard in my mind, above the dirge, in the singing wind. "*Yes-come-yes-come.*"

"Marl," said Elmoleonard.

I stepped toward the skiff but felt their arms around me, a dozen arms holding me against my desire to join the Sirens, tying me to themselves as if a mast. I screamed and the ghosts screamed. My screams shook them and they quivered around me, the ocean itself trembled, the ice fell, formed, called, then fell again. The sky collapsed and the island before us melted into the sea. Over the tank, the swirl of forms faded into haze, a fog, a simple mist, and then was gone. I saw the baleen whales working in the ocean beyond the membrane nets, heard their moans and the skree of the dolphins skittering. Then I felt the oddest thing. I wanted to see birds. I whispered, "The moon needs birds."

XX

Ermanmelville did not have accommodations beyond his own, so we took the elevator back to our ship. I noticed then that Elmoleonard had shed their biosphere to hold me back from the ghosts. They were all quite wet and busy preening each other, emitting a musky stink they clearly could not control, for which they apologized.

"Most of us don't enjoy the water," several of them said.

"Did you save my life just then?" said I.

"Yes, Marl. Did you expect you might live on a momentary ice floe?"

"I had no expectations at all," I said. "Is that what happened to the Nutian?"

"The Nutian?"

"Who preceded me here."

"No. The Nutian do not see them, Marl. They see only ice and mist."

"Why do you suppose that?"

The Pet stopped preening, all them, in unison, and responded in unison. "Are we being interrogated about the Nutian?" They went back into motion, their hands smoothing each other. "We told you already. Really, we should go now, Marl."

"I need to stay I little longer," I said.

There came a smell, an odor that reminded me of being at my mother's breast, though I did not possess the original memory. "We have developed an affection for you," they said.

"You would develop an affection for anything, no doubt," I said.

"Not the Nutian."

"We are all Nutian," I said.

"And not any*thing*. Any*one*, possibly. Is that an observation or a criticism, Marl?" Together with a pungent, almost skeptical odor, their voices came to me in chorus, almost in tune. I must have given off a questioning odor for the Pet paused again. "One begins to sing here," they said.

"Yes, the tune in the wind."

"The cetaceans believe that the ghosts of their ancestors are here; that they come to work with them, to commiserate, that the ghosts taught them that song."

"And the Pets?"

"We believe that the ocean is alive and the mist and ice, even the air, is its consciousness. Before the first probes, you might know, the gap between the sea and sky was much smaller and the atmosphere methane. Check the intuo-logs."

"I'm aware of the moon's history," I said.

"For us the ghosts have a smell. Did you smell them?"

"No."

Elmoleonard emitted a gracious odor. "It is the same as our smell for *gift*. Isn't that an odd coincidence?"

"I've encountered more unusual ones."

"Yet *Gift Moon* is a Nutian name. It's a coincidence of great irony."

I didn't understand and had to ask them to explain.

"Well, Marl," intoned someone in the furry horde, "it would seem that the ocean realizes that its ghosts are no gift at all, and so like the Gift Moon itself, no gift for those of us who work it. In fact, likely, it was never given to anyone, but taken."

"Abstract nonsense," I said.

"Marl," crooned the beast, "you are trying to find the stolen fish freighter? We are trying to help you."

XXI

So there was much more explaining, if only about *irony*, a word I'd never before heard, an ancient homan word which pointed out a contradiction underlying some apparent truth.

It seemed I was having many mysteries solved for me, at least very theoretically, though none of the ones I had come to solve. "I fail to see the relevance," I said to Elmoleonard. "Unless you are implying that the moon is involved on some intellectual level with a conspiracy against the Nutian."

"Could it not have chosen not to show itself to you at all?"

"There are far too many negatives in that question," I said to the Pet. But I had been aroused, you see. Lead around. Confused. Disarmed. If the Pet was a subtle group, so too it was loyal and valuable, for there it was in front of me, an administrator of the Gift Moon. I was there to find out what it was taking apart and what it was holding together. I needed more time.

"Nonetheless," I finally said to them, "I perceive no danger here."

"The pirates, Marl."

"And what of Ermanmelville then, and the pirates?"

The Pet gave a collective heave. "Ermanmelville will be safer if the Nutian Ambassador is not here."

"And the pirates know I am here."

"Yes," said the Pet. "Likely."

"All the more reason, then, why I should stay." For whoever the pirates were, if they knew of my presence amid the fleet then it was possible, even likely, that they had an agent among the cetaceans.

"We suppose it would be selfish of us to plead for our own precious livelihood," crooned the Pet. "After all, *survive and contribute*, does contain the word *survive*."

It was the first time since my initial encounter with the creature that I recoiled from it, though I found myself, as well, reeling from information, or misinformation, but reeling.

"If you'll excuse me, I need to think," I told them and retired to my tiny bio-chamber, needing time alone, time to contemplate, though I did not get it because no sooner had my abode settled around me when L entered and I found myself torn between my loneliness and desire to be left alone, drawn achingly toward her, both resenting and demanding of myself that I do what I was sent to do, contribute, for lack of a better word, my duty.

In a moment she was upon me and I was within her and it took me some time to find any intellect amid the chaos of pleasure; each time as she found me settling into comfort, rhythm, she moved, she changed the dance of carnal havoc, gripping me in the ache of love, of desire, split in the mania of simultaneous have and want, a razor of satisfaction and dissatisfaction. Yet in time I accepted it, gave over to it, and in refusing to fight it, I then found myself there behind the waiting. I found her eyes.

"L," I said, "how could the cetaceans be unhappy? How can anyone be unhappy?"

"How could anyone be happy, Marl?"

I concentrated, then released my concentration. Something else came. "Where did Elmoleonard learn those words?"

"Like *irony*?"

"Yes."

"I brought them. We keep them in the Wild Zone."

"Keep them?"

"We write."

"Write?"

"And read."

She brought me to climax. I gasped next to her, though already I felt her rising to me again and me, as well, impossibly beginning to be again aroused. The silk of her down, her soft breasts and blazing eyes, her smell, her *smell!* The deadly, deep smell of her sex. Yet if she were there to confuse me, then why was Elmoleonard so forthcoming? Why did they save my life when I could have disappeared as easily as my First-Nutian predecessors?

"I know what you're thinking, Marl, and we were not involved with the freighter," said L.

"The cetaceans are unhappy," I managed to say.

"Maybe you are thinking too much about the freighter," she said, bringing me up again. "Maybe it has little or nothing to do with fish."

"Who would hijack a billion fish if they did not want fish?"

"Yes," she said. "Who? And why take them to Mars?"

"Then you know they were sent to Mars."

"You said they were, Marl. We know what you told us."

But now she had me within her again, in the rage of ecstasy. Even so, she took my forearm and with her long nail drew figures along it that she said represented sounds. She made a word out of the sounds. *Fuck.* She laughed. She trilled. "Marl," she whispered in my ear, "this cannot be about fish."

These were the last words I heard before our vessel began to scream and a horrible thudding reverberated against its sides. Before I could rise the ship writhed and flung us to the floor. I heard the ripping and tearing of flesh as the walls around us began to seep with plasma. L took my hand. "Hurry," she said. "The pirates. They are here."

XXII

We groped and slid on our hands and knees, slipping from my convulsing chamber into the bleeding hold where Elmoleonard lumbered in frenzy toward the elevator.

"Your sphere," I yelled to them.

"No time. No time," they chorused as L drew me to them and the elevator surged, then stopped, then surged again, as if we were some leaden substance in the belly of a whale. When we reached the deck, the dock and tanks were in chaos. I had forgotten my leathers and goggles and immediately I shivered uncontrollably in the chill of the cold, salt sea, under the deafening scream of the dolphins, the moaning of the baleen whales, the black backs of Orcas moving among them in an ocean already filled with blood. On the horizon a line a mile long rose and fell from the water, a hundred thousand dolphins rising and falling in unison, like an avalanche in the sea.

"Help," I said almost in prayer. "Allies."

Elmoleonard said, "No."

Now Ermanmelville, too, was upon the tiny deck and the group of us huddled there in the center of the rage. The umbilical elevator burst open, spilling a million fish into the sky, a rain of fish into the sea of blood, falling into the chaos as the membrane nets burst, too, torn by the square jaws of sperm whales, the dolphin workers fleeing into the ocean around. The mouths of the Orcas surrounded us, their teeth as long as my arms, their high pitched echoes skreeing, maddening.

"There is no hope," I whispered to Elmoleonard.

"I'm afraid not, Marl," they said.

In the sea beyond now the freed dolphins mixed and screamed with attacking ones in the putrid water, breaching among the carcasses of the dead baleens as the Orcas tore into the whale flesh. From among them, a giant, gray head arose, almost white against the bloody sea. I felt L's hand in mine as a huge beast rose from the ocean in front of us, rose to the deck and opened its jaws, its tongue as purple as a heart, its teeth as white as the ice of the Gift Moon.

XXIII

I kept hold of L's hand as the jaws of the white creature opened upon us. We were not eaten. Quite obviously we were not eaten. How could I have died? I'm the narrator! (Though I've now read hundreds of books where I am obviously supposed to feel suspense about whether or not the author survived. As I have said, books are full of unimaginable contradictions).

We were carried, rather, in the jaws of the beast, fed by its own undulating breath, held, wrapped in its tongue, and in time passed to the mouth of another creature, and then yet another, each time expecting to be swallowed like so much bird-like regurgitation, but yet never swallowed, only passed from behemoth to behemoth, mouth to mouth, until we sat before an Orca, though not quite an Orca, a beast with modified flippers much like Elmoleonard's lad and the many dolphins who worked the phlegm nets. The animal's black face was carved, almost featured, with expressive eyes, a cultured mouth and sculpted jaw. It lay on its side, in a fold of tongue, its dazzling white belly exposed to us as it sucked smoke from a container half-full of cloudy water.

The beast did not speak in chirps and whistles, but in an unrecognizable language uttered from the back of its throat, a sound both high-pitched and guttural. I was startled when L, shivering and wet, and clinging to my side, responded in kind.

"It is an ancient tongue from my region," she said to me, her wet hands caressing my nape, though more to comfort herself than me. "It was called German."

"How remarkable you are," I said to her.

"You have yet to know how remarkable," she whispered. She turned to the Orca. "I wish to know the fate of my family," she said.

The creature before us paused and let out smoke. "What are you?" it said.

"Cue me," I said to L. "Let me speak." Part of my intuitive skills included the ability to absorb and extrapolate spoken language on the basis of central structures, another reason I proved essential to the First-Nutian whose intuitive abilities did not give them easy access to the eccentricities of oral communication. I suppressed my curiosity, and suspicion, as to how both my companions spoke a language from before the Return and within twenty minutes of translation and counter-translation found I could begin to speak the German in a rudimentary form. Our host was female and though she had a long, complicated, Orca name, she suggested we call her the Queen of Hearts.

"The stolen ship," the creature in front of us said. "What have you learned?"

"I won't be interrogated," I said to her. "Nor am I afraid to die."

"You're life is not at stake," she said.

"Then what is at stake?" I said.

"Nor your Pet's," said the Orca.

"We are not family," L said.

"You are not a colony?" asked the Queen of Hearts.

"No," I replied.

"You are homan," she said. "Landhoman. We are homan. What are you?" she said to L.

"We are all Nutian," I said.

"I am from Elmoleonard," said L.

"We know them," the Orca said. She inhaled from her pipe and held her breath, peering at us through a squint until raising her head to exhale. The creature beneath us sagged.

"Are you responsible this carnage?" I said to the Queen of Hearts.

"We are carnivores."

"This was not hunting."

"No?" said the creature. "It is our nature."

"Is it your nature to speak ancient homan? What kind of world do you think we shall have if we are all thrashing about eating each other?" I said to her. "Even if you choose not to contribute there are yet plenty of fish to eat on this moon."

"The fish cause sterility in mammals," the Queen of Hearts said.

"Nonsense."

"It is true," she said. "Why are there none of us left in the oceans of Home? Why are there so few Landhoman?"

"The problems of pollution and sterility began years before the Return. How do the dolphins who work the nets here propagate?"

"They do not. They are cloned."

Whatever my fear and misgiving, the creature in front of me had been quite rational and forthright, despite her so very recent display of violence and bloodlust. These creatures, the toothed cetaceans on this moon, seemed to have constructed a rationale for who they were and what they did. It was my job to bring them back to the simple sense of contribution and survival. The conversation had hardly proceeded logically and now many issues were confused. It had been my own fault, though I forgave myself; the context did not encourage clear thinking. Nonetheless, that was my job. If in the past I'd seen myself as a kind of transportable glue that helped secure the harmony among species in the solar system, now, more than ever, I felt how dear that harmony was and how important I had become to it. Yet I'd never before encountered this kind of encircling dialogue, this thought-out blend of philosophy and purported fact, which justified their antagonism to the beauty of how we had evolved.

L, who till then clung to me with adhesion, began to relax and preen her fur. The creature, the Queen of Hearts, bowed slightly and offered her the pipe and, surprisingly, L took it up. "My family," L said.

"Please," said the Queen of Hearts, "it will calm you, as well as our gracious host who absorbs the smoke through his tongue." She gestured to the walls, which rose, exposing teeth, the tongue beneath us rolling like a waterbed. The Queen of Hearts turned her head to me. "It is symbiosis," she said. "The Nutian never had a monopoly."

I sat down cross-legged before the creature, as did L, and we smoked. The concoction made me slightly giddy at first, light-headed, then settled into clarity, if not more rational then certainly more vivid.

"So you resort to eating your own kind," I said to the Queen of Hearts. I felt that if I could trigger the creature's rashness I could circle back to the problem of the missing freighter.

"They are not *us*, Marl," she said. "You are Marl, yes?"

I nodded slightly. "You seem to know enough," I said, stretching my diplomacy, reminding myself that it would gain me nothing to antagonize her. I bowed my head slightly as I returned the pipe, mimicking the gesture she'd made while passing it to L.

"We have fed on the baleen for hundreds of thousands of years," the Orca said. "Besides, they are Nutian cows."

I understood the reference. I'd seen cows, or versions of them, in the Wild Zones. "And what of the Pets?" I said.

"The marsupials?" She turned to L, studying her again. "You are homan," said the Orca.

"Once," said L.

"From Home," the Queen of Hearts said to L, then raised her head and whistled and clicked. Within minutes a dolphin came in between our hosts teeth, leaving my leathers at my feet and exchanging some high-pitched dialogue with the Queen of Hearts. "They are dead," she said. "I am sorry. Casualties of war."

L's expression did not change; she simply clutched my arm tightly with her hand.

"Of war?" I said.

"Revolution," said the Orca.

"I do not know the words."

"Conflict," L said.

"With a purpose," said the Orca. "Marl, we wish to return Home."

XXIV

I allowed a long silence. "The oceans are no longer saline enough," I finally said.

"You might be surprised," she said.

"And what will you eat if the fish sterilize mammals?"

"We shall take the baleen with us."

"And what will they eat?"

"The krill is not poisoned," said the Orca. "Not here. Likely, not there."

It became very obvious to me that these cetaceans did not hijack the fish freighter, unless this was a very sophisticated misdirection. It would have been much easier to have slain me, and more wise. Why permit me to survive and expose them? Further, though the freighters could easily support creatures of their size, adapted with air space for mammals—that was likely how the first of them were transported here as youngsters when they were much smaller, obviously for some contribution from which they had now seemed to distance themselves—the umbilical elevators were not big enough to transport the larger, full-grown cetaceans to the ship. That would require biotechnology. But I did not possess that. Then again, maybe the smaller dolphins had already moved out in the vanguard. It still left my survival here confusing, as well as the fact that the course of the stolen freighter was traced to Mars, where it disappeared, hardly a fit environment for fish *or* dolphins. For lack of a better phrase, it seemed I sat in front of a very large plate of red herrings.

"How do you expect to accomplish any of your goals through violence?" I said.

"It brought you," she said.

"To what end?"

"What do you know of the freighter?" the creature said.

"As little as you, or less," I said.

We sat quietly then. The Orca smoked and then we passed the pipe around. L moved closer to me and began to massage my shoulders, pressing her chest to my back.

"What if I report what I have seen here?" I said.

"Yes," the Queen of Hearts responded. "What if you do? Shall we find that the Nutian are capable of reprisal?" She shifted her gaze from me to L, then returned her eye contact to me. "You are homan, Marl. We are homan."

"Nutian," I insisted.

"But we are not First-Nutian. You are not. We are hoping that you will come to see that, and help us."

L was almost dry now and we sat, entwined. I felt her pressing upon me as a kind of grieving, yet even in that horrible context I could not help but feel distracted and aroused by her petting. "L," I whispered. "Please. Let me speak."

The Orca looked on, almost bemused. "The Pets are strange," she said, which brought L to a pause.

"What do you know of the freighter?" I said to the Queen of Hearts.

"The Krtz?" she said.

L began to caress me again, but I held her wrists, for I recalled that sound from my initial meeting with Elmoleonard.

"Ktz," I said to L.

"The Krtz," the Orca said again. "The holy one of Mars."

"Holy."

"The reason for everything. If it is on Mars, then it has to do with Krtz."

"That's where the freighter was traced," I told her.

"Then you have a corroboration," she said. "If vague."

"Have you kept this from me?" I said to L.

"A myth?" said L. "A bed time story?"

"She is correct," said the Orca. "It is little more than that. A symbol. But it's said that symbols go a long way on Mars."

"A man?" I asked. "A woman? An Indigo?"

"We are alone on an ocean moon," the Orca said. "It is interesting how isolated we homan are from each other." The Orca shifted, raised herself, then settled again. "It is time for water," she said.

"Who is Krtz?" I demanded.

"You are homan, Marl. We are homan," said the whale. "Help us."

When I said nothing the creature said, "We shall return you to your ship."

"Survive and contribute," I said.

XV

The Orca, the Queen of Hearts, gazed at us quixotically, then moved quickly to the back jaw of our host and slipped from its maw into the sea. Instantly the huge animal wrapped us in its tongue and plunged upward. It would seem we were quite close to the umbilical elevator at the Port of Friends, for in not much time we found ourselves deposited on its dock where we quickly ducked inside. There, Elmoleonard's cetacean boy awaited. I wasted no time and explained to him the Pet's fate.

The boy stood silently for a little while, then squealed, "Thank you. I am free then."

"We are all always free," I said.

"Free to contribute?" he said.

"Yes," I said. "What other freedom is there?"

He lifted his head and nodded at the air. "The open sea," said the boy.

"You will join the revolt?"

"The open sea," the dolphin boy said again.

"A war of all against all," I said to him.

"I am not a Pet. Not Landhoman. Not Nutian. I am a dolphin."

"You *are* Nutian," I said. "Look at you."

The boy looked to L who sat alone, massaging herself, her eyelids like frail shades, like mists obscuring twin moons. "What will you do?" he squealed to her.

"Mars," she said, not lifting an eyelid.

"There are plenty more fishing fleets here," I said to the two of them. "There are dolphins," I said to the boy, "and Pets," to L.

L opened her eyes. "I'm afraid," she said.

I had expected a more rational protest. In front of such simple emotion I was speechless.

"Weren't you afraid today?" she said.

"Of death? Of course not."

"Of hate," said L.

The boy interrupted us. "I'm going to leave now," he said. "I wish you warmth and affection," he said to L. But to me he offered only a shy smile. He lumbered to the water hatch, turned slowly to survey his old home, then turned to me again. "Luck," he said.

Such an odd concept. Luck. I met his eyes. "Survive," I uttered, but could not utter more. I said it again. "Survive."

He nodded and dove into the sea.

XXVI

Then I felt L at my back, her hands upon my neck and head, her breast pushing into my shoulders and the heat of her sex against my spine. Beneath a fatigue deeper than bone deep arose my desire and soon she sat astride me; I was thoughtless beyond time, a rush of avarice, lust, passion, union. Beyond pleasure, this was corruption, an erosion of duty, self, humanity, and I, a burning, expanding star, burning, expanding, then caving in upon myself in brown despair. Naked on this moon of ice, of ghosts, of blood, I had never been more vulnerable, and yet, that she did not betray me, made my trust more vulnerable still, a soul colonized by desire. She did not even sit upon me. She swarmed.

"L," I said, fighting for sense. "There is work to be done."

"Don't leave me," she said.

"You are dangerous to me."

"Yes."

"What are you, L?" I said.

"Without me, the moon will take you. The ghosts will take you. The mist will turn your blood to ice."

"My blood."

"To ice."

"To ice. My eyes. My blood."

I cannot explain what then became of me. I became something of fur. I was the odor of semen in her nose. She was inside me. I was nothing, the last refuge of anything like myself, cold, distant, reptilian. There, incubating inside my skin, I found one moment leading to another and there I found identity. Marl. Me. Survive. Contribute. Feeling that she'd held me on the edge too long, I feigned repose, then came. Soon I was fighting sleep.

"No wonder you people never got anything done," I whispered.

XXVII

"God is excess," she said.

"God?"

When I came to we took the elevator to my orbiting ship. We fucked from Europa to Mars. She wrote upon my skin. We wrote upon the walls of the ship as it slid beneath our fingers, our words the scars of consciousness upon its lungs. Our bodies spelled bliss as dark and restless as rain and between the lines of this ancient twisting, everything, even bliss, fell into duplicity; the world, the real, the obvious danced under our skin like illusion beneath magic. Did she know she was a spy? Did she know that I knew? Did it matter?

XXVIII

If you are terrestrial, Landhoman as say the cetaceans, then there is something of Mars in your essence. It is hard to imagine Home in the days of its continents, land masses teaming with beasts that walked, crawled, flew; cities stuffed with homan beings moving about inside their machines. It seems unimaginable. But as the Nutian say, the body forgets nothing, the mind everything. We reside deep inside ourselves and never even know we are there.

I suppose this was the draw of Mars for the first Indigos, if not, as well, the first homans whose machines still lay about the planet in rusted decadence. Once, before the Return, giant mirrors orbited the surface, enlarging the sun, and giant smokestacks stoked by nuclear fission spewed carbon dioxide into the air; a great irony of our species that we tried to bring Mars to life using the same machine technology that was strangling Home with greenhouse heat. This is when the first domes, the first tent cities were erected, when came the first polar melt, the first flowing streams in billions of years, the first green, the first rain.

All of that was already in collapse before the Return. Now a viscous membrane encircled Mars, magnifying light, breathing in carbon dioxide and exhaling nitrogen and oxygen like a plant cell. Summer temperatures on the highest volcanoes near the equator reached well above freezing, though the air at those heights was yet too thin to breathe. At the lower levels of the planet you could breathe the air, though often you needed a dust mask, and better yet a dry suit equipped with water tubing. Ground water swells which once dissipated into the thin, icy air now flowed into craters where oases formed along the rims and Idigo tribes fought for hegemony.

The southern pole was carbon ice and most of the southern hemisphere high, cratered plateau but for one giant basin, but it was only a matter of time before the water-ice of the north pole melted enough to turn the low lying northern hemisphere into a shallow ocean.

Contrary to what homans believed before the Return, and if you can believe the Nutian, though there seems little reason to doubt them on this, very few known solar systems have developed terrestrial planets. Most star systems, if they have developed planets at all, contain one or two gas giants with oblique orbits very close to their suns. If Home is a miracle amid a billion stars, so too is Mars, if not, as well, Venus and Mercury, though the Nutian had as yet done little to change these inner planets. As the Nutian say, there is time.

XXIX

Our destination was the umbilical elevator that ran from a stationary orbit satellite to a base at the top of the tallest Martian volcano, in fact the tallest mountain in the solar system, stretching almost twenty thousand meters above the plain and sitting northwest of a string of mountains, three of them quite large, which ran northeast to southwest across the Martian equator. The Nutian names for these landmarks were not pronounceable, but the Indigos called the largest mountain Olympus, the string the Tharsis Bulge, and each volcano by yet another exotic name from a homan language long dead, even before the Return.

"Ancient Greek," said L. Of course, we could barely converse unless locked onto each other like dogs. "They were the first homan scientists. The mountains are named after Gods."

"Non-existent beings held accountable for existence," I said.

"You sound like a Nutian catechism, Marl."

"And what is a catechism? Am I to assume there were ancient telescopes?"

"How far back do you want to go?"

"To Ancient Greece, I suppose, when homan scientists who could not see the features of Mars named those features after non-existent entities."

"Mars itself is a Latin word," she said. "Another God."

"Yes," I said, "the famous Latins."

"Romans," said L. "Mars is after the Greek, Ares, the God of War."

"War," I said. "Am I to perceive some kind of synchronicity?"

"I'm proud of you for noticing, Marl."

"You are proud of me."

"But it would be much more foreboding if I meant it that way, or if it were true."

"You are so guileless," I said.

"You know better," said L.

"So it's symbolic," I said to her, using one of my new words. "Mars. War."

"Prophetic is better," said L.

As you see, these conversations took place within an undeniable, if inane, rhythm, as if our banter were the only way for us to tell each other apart, and the moments when we were not upon each other more like the time a fish might spend out of water, gasping on air. Much as I imagined the Pets themselves lived, we became each other's element.

"When homans first developed the technology to view the planets, Marl, they used the ancient languages of Greek and Latin, partly from deference and tradition, but for religious reasons, too. At the time they were all of a religion that kept those languages alive. The Arabians mapped the stars before the Europeans, so the stars had Arab names."

"What's a European?" I said.

"It was the land mass around my Zone. Every culture had its own names for the planets and stars, in their own languages, usually closely tied with their religious beliefs"

"Sounds like a lot of chaos," I said.

"Spoken like an amphibian."

"What is religion?"

"God stories," she said.

"Stories?"

"Soon, Marl, you'll know more about them than you want to know."

"What is the average lifespan in a Wild Zone?" I said to her. "Twenty? Twenty-five?"

"Maybe," she said.

"And how old are you?" I said.

"I don't know. Maybe nineteen."

"By the Nutian! I am ten times older than you."

"And you know ten times less," she said.

"You learned a lot of worthless nonsense very quickly," I told her.

"We have things saved from before the Return. In writing."

"You keep it?"

"Yes, and read it. And when your life expectancy is twenty-five, you learn fast."

"But why?" I said. "Why bother?"

"To preserve it, Marl. For a different future."

"So you didn't just leave the Wild Zone to save your life," I said, "but to disseminate nonsense."

"That's right, Marl. I'm a subversive. I'm a writing teacher. And you have been contaminated."

"You cannot be a subversive," I reminded L. "There is no such thing, because there is nothing to subvert Your information is either fabricated or trivial."

"You're so kind," she said.

"All information is."

"That's why you're out here trying to gather it."

"You have no idea why I am out here," I said.

"If I did, would it go badly for me?"

"Everything is permitted," I reminded her.

"Even revolution and war?"

"They are anachronisms. They die out on their own."

"Everything dies, Marl. What is important is how we live."

"However briefly, if you are in a Wild Zone," said I.

"However briefly," she said. "What I find so confounding, is that it is impossible to find any of it meaningful, life, that is, and equally impossible to see it as meaningless."

"Look at what is in front of your face," I said to her. "The universe has become a living thing. Enjoy your part."

She stroked my face, held it before her eyes. She was making fun of me, but the way a child does who doesn't understand and in her ignorance assumes superiority. Yet without a doubt, L was one of the most interesting creatures I had met in years. For the first time, in all of my inter-planetary travel, I did not hibernate, but during the whole trip talked and fucked and, to humor her, learned to write. Sometimes I spent hours watching her move upon herself, stroking and preening, other times we simply lay next to each other, innocuously petting in a kind of tactile bliss. I often found myself incapable of self conception without imagining her near me, feeling a need more visceral and self-serving than love, more obsessive and passionate, yet all the while knowing that very soon I would have to do something with her, do something about her, probably soon after landing on Mars, for I could not carry out my duties with her draped over me with her mind-draining sensuality and trivial revolution.

XXX

On Mars there were some First-Nutian, but they occupied a lab near the north pole. They did not move well on land and the weak gravity of Mars, a third less than that of Home, created more, not fewer, difficulties for them. Thus the evermore importance of water. But as our ship approached the red planet I felt, for the first time, a prescient nostalgia for the northern hemisphere of Mars, a longing for land, for the planet that was once all land and nothing else; Mars the red, virgin desert.

"It's natural, Marl," said L, as we prepared to enter the umbilical shaft. "You're a land animal."

"Landhoman?" I said.

"You don't like the term."

"It's divisive," I said. "We are Nutian.

"What happens if you say 'I am not Nutian,'" said L. "What does that change?"

"Nothing," I said.

"Write it down," said L.

"Write what down?"

"Anything. Either one."

"Don't be silly," I said.

A massive Pet, looking much like a pile of foxes, met us at the base atop Olympus, some 26 Kilometers above the Martian datum. She stood almost three meters tall and almost equally as wide. I had come to referring to them in the feminine because all of them were, at core, mothers, despite their proclivity to take on long, male names, in this case, Elronhubbard. She swarmed upon herself madly and smelled horrible, like the sweat of a thousand things that all wanted something from each other. In fact, I recognized her odor from a journey I had once made to the Ort Cloud, a long and agonizing trip I took over fifty Home years ago to pacify the comet sifters, homan space workers who had declared independence. I traveled for almost two years to meet the dissidents on Charon, the moon that danced with Pluto (planetoids bathed magically in sunlight as dim as a night on earth under a full moon, the sun, at mid-day, a ragged yellow wink in the black distance) to notify them that it was fine, they could be as independent as they pleased.

Their disappointment was dismal. And, to put it as L might, the irony of my presence quite utter. I had been sent only to tell them that their independence was meaningless. It was well within the Nutian temperament to permit them to rot there on the edge of nothing, organized around some idea, raging at space. Was it kindness or cynicism which put me two years in space to tell them, "Good luck?" They had organized themselves around some vague principle concerning the unique individuality of each self. Wonderful. "That's wonderful," I said. "Without Nutian bio-technology and supplies, how do you plan on feeding your *selves* out here?"

Not to go on about it, but their ambassador had been this creature before us now, Elronhubbard, though there had been much less, or should I say fewer, of her in the Ort Cloud days. I had felt then that she had been remiss in her sympathy, though the demise of Elmoleonard and Ermanmelville on the Gift Moon had given me some perspective on the delicacy of Pet diplomacy during what, in an emotional context, and without the long vision of Nutian perspective, might seem like a crisis. Still, she was the prototype of why I distrusted Pets and I did not like her.

"Marl," she odiferated ambiguously. There clearly some commotion in the colony over L who laconically swarmed upon me as I stood before my host.

"I know you, at least some of you," I said. "From the Ort Zone."

Unlike Elmoleonard who iterated and odorated amid a chorus of chaos, often quibbling among herself, Elronhubbard sounded out from somewhere in the mother-core, much less homan in tone, a chorus of mutual, whispered cooing.

"A sad end to senseless commotion," I said. Over time, new colonies of sifters were added, the dissenters ignored, and over a few decades everything was back to normal. Likely there were small bands of independent homan out there in that black, empty region, eking out dim lives in bio-caves.

"Defeated in the end more by emptiness than anything," Elronhubbard said. "We couldn't but admire them."

"Less admiration and more guidance might have helped," I said.

"We offered to incorporate some of them at the end."

"Undoubtedly," I said.

"They were very—" the creature hesitated, "—could you understand this, Marl?—individualistic."

"You mean self-serving."

"You won't find it much different here," she said.

"There is nothing here now," I said very directly. I had found that with most Pets you needed to be quite direct or you might find yourself in a sea of digression. "When the planet is aqua-formed, things will change."

The Pet heaved, then came forward adroitly. On the Ghost Moon, water permitted the Nutian to manipulate density, as in the biomass of our space ships, much like the way a cat makes itself heavier when it sleeps and lighter when it leaps. That technology did not apply well on terrestrial planets and here on Mars the gravity was just over a third that of Home. Elronhubbard less swarmed around herself than glided, and when she lifted to move she had the appearance of a furry dance.

"Homan accommodations here are not good," Elronhubbard said, extending a paw. "As you know, we Pets tend to make furniture of ourselves. Your friend might be more comfortable with us."

L immediately emitted a laden, complex odor. For a moment, I, too, was transported by memory to the recent horrific events on the Gift Moon.

"Poor child," Elronhubbard said.

"You're aware then?" I said.

"She just told us," said Elronhubbard.

"I am sorry for your friends," I said to her.

"We live long lives," she said. "We are not eternal."

L slipped from my side and began to dance around the Pet, motion around motion; in the light gravity it made me dizzy.

"What do you know of the ship, then?" I said to the creature in front of me. "Do you know of the Krtz?"

Elronhubbard did not respond, but expanded, so much so that I had to step back from the swirling explosion of creatures, some dancing, some hurling about each other in unfurled, weightless fury. Instantly L was among them, and instantly indistinguishable. When they quieted, when they settled, she was gone.

"L," I said. I should have been paying more attention to her.

"She is among us," Elronhubbard said.

"You have taken her. L," I said. "L!" But she didn't answer.

"It's too late," the creature said, her odor like sweet liquor. "She has chosen."

XXXI

On land, the Nutian travel by animal. As I have said, they are sel-dom in a hurry. Regardless, they were loathe to travel terrestrially, preferring the buoyancy of water, yet when they did, it could not be accomplished for any distance without water-suits which kept their skin moist. Here in the mountainous region of Mars, flying was quite popular among the Indigos and local tribes near Olympus took wing on the backs of huge dragonflies, each tribe and even tribelet identify-ing with and mounting a favored, specific species. They trained the insects, flew them, and fought each other, airborne, over trade corri-dors throughout the region. Casual air travel was almost impossible.

Among the various European tribes in the area, French, Swiss, Lux, I headed for the nearest hamlet, inhabited by a group who called themselves *Austrians*. Keeping a habitat as close as they did to the spaceport they had some history of dealing with the Nutian, among others. It was not a long walk and the thin air was quite dry despite a significant snow pack. Snow was more common here, on Mars, than on Home, where it accumulated only in the winter on the highest peaks of certain Wild Zones.

I descended from the top of Olympus on a narrow path that dipped beneath vertical walls of crystalline snow, then rose against red cliffs, only to dip again and then rise, sometimes into open space, the diminutive sun winking above in the pink Martian sky. Much like a First-Nutian, I wore a water suit, very similar to the leathers I wore on the Ghost Moon, a kind of living, breathing skin with a circulatory system regulated by my own body heat, though this suit kept my skin moist, as well, transforming carbon dioxide into breathable oxygen and synthesizing my own hydrogen and oxygen into drinking water. I could access either one through my sand mask which connected to the suit at the waist, and in that thin, dry air I used as much as I could produce.

I traveled light. The Indigos, when not fearsome, were notoriously hospitable, and already I was quite certain that I'd spotted some on several occasions, moving above me like quick, blue shadows on their silver and black boards on which they surfed elusively between rock and cave and cliff like nightmares across the snow.

As I bounded along in the light gravity, I found myself, in moments, missing L. As much as I knew that we would have had to part there on Mars, I was struck by visceral loss. Conversely, my distaste for Elronhubbard was profound.

Over the years I had passed through the lives of several mates and countless lovers, seen my children grow up, grow old, and die. I had become a solitary man, at peace with my survival as well as my contributions. Experience had taught me that what was once conceived as commonplace might very well, in time, be seen as extraordinary, and what was once impossible might become commonplace. Yet whatever one thought of homan sexuality, it was apparently unique. The species of other worlds seemed either to practice their sensuality in hoards like the Pets, or barely at all, like the First-Nutian. Perhaps it was the Nutian cells inside me, but it had been decades since I'd felt the need for anyone or suffered over their loss. Now I felt both.

I descended onto a green plateau where an Austrian village of about a hundred huts sat under one impressive cliff and overlooked another, before the long, gradual descent down Olympus Mons, the red desert stretching to the three volcanoes in the distance. Eventually I wanted a horse, which like the Indigos themselves, were tall and willowy, capable of moving overland in great bounds, but the landscape here on the mountain made them much less useful than on the plains; other derivative species from earth, like llamas, donkeys, and goats, which were more sure-footed and built more for agility than speed, were commonly used as pack animals, but in terms of riding they were difficult to control. Unlike on the plains, the people here were not migratory and raised and ate goat and mutton which grazed the plateau during the long summer and fed on harvested grass and corn during the winter which was dry and bitter cold.

My approach had been advertised. A woman met me at the village edge. She was tall, over a head taller than me, and quite thin and pale. Under her woolen hood and cloak, both dark gray, her face and hands glistened like the slightest hint of turquoise over alabaster or pearl, a remarkable contrast against the red cliffs, the white snow, the pink sky. Her eyes were large and light brown, almost tan, like polished stone. She did not appear young, but beyond that here age was indiscernible.

She greeted me in what I now knew to be German, the language that the Queen of Hearts spoke on Ghost Moon, Gift Moon. In the past I had always managed with visceral Nutian or sign language, as well as what I had, till then, regarded as homan tongue but have since learned to be a primitive form of English, once the language of several pre-Return nations, the language I am writing in now, however poorly.

Regardless, she could not have expected me to know German beyond *Guten tag* and appeared surprised when I responded in kind to her queries as to my origin and destination. I said, quite plainly, my name was Marl and I was from Home. A fish ship had left Gift Moon and disappeared, last traced heading here, to Mars.

She could not have appeared less interested. She placed a thin hand over her lips.

"You speak German," she said.

"I learned some on Gift Moon," I said.

"Europa," she said, using the pre-Return name. "With a good eye, you can see it from here." Her voice was both scratchy and dancing.

"I learned it from an Orca," I said, "and a Pet."

"The fish are speaking German on Europa?" Two dragonfliers approached from above and hovered behind her, an amazing sight. The insects themselves, luminous with color, were some five meters long, their quadrupled wings, stretching out double that in width, sizzled deafeningly. The riders perched behind their heads like phantoms. The woman simply raised her hand and they rose vertically and zipped away.

"Remarkable," I said.

"I would find talking fish quite remarkable," she said.

"They're not fish," I said, carrying on. I noticed that she wore an amulet that hung from twine at her collarbone. Like L's, it depicted a winged creature, reptilian, exhaling fire. "Orca are mammals, a kind of cetacean. In fact they call themselves seahoman."

"That's interesting," she said. "If they can speak German they could probably fly a fish ship."

"To Mars?" I said.

She simply nodded, raising an eyebrow.

"Have you heard of someone named the Krtz?"

She placed her long hands inside her robe. "Are you hungry?" she asked.

I followed her into the village to a hut she kept near its edge. Despite the oddity of my attire I did not draw much attention. My carriage, my size, and the quickness of my movement, however unaccustomed I was to Martian gravity, displayed that I was not a First-Nutian. Besides, it was midday and people took advantage of the sun, working corn and grain fields, shearing sheep, drying meat. Indigo cultures generally fell somewhere on a spectrum of hunting, gathering, and agriculture in some combination and traced themselves to a pre-Return exodus from Home. They harbored, almost trans-culturally among all their uncountable tribes, a rejection of machine technology, however contradictory one might find that, given that their arrival here, as well as the original transformation of the planet, were both by means of pre-Return mechanical science. Continuing in this convoluted line of reasoning, they had become radical advocates of preserving Mars rather than terra-forming it further, let alone aqua-forming it. Thus the Nutian, with whom they had been originally sympathetic, were now considered antagonists and the Indigos, who fought each other constantly, were quite good at antagonism.

It was among the Indigos that I first learned of the concepts of *government* and *nationhood*, things they universally despised without having the slightest clue as to what they were. Instead of everyone simply just doing their own work, minding their own business and leaving everyone else alone, Indigo tribes perpetuated complicated, internal systems to prevent an individual or group from dominating or fighting with another, apparently afraid that intra-tribal affairs might become as battle-ridden as extra-tribal ones. Among these Austrians, only adult females could *own* things, like huts and tools, and even children, to own meaning that you have complete responsibility for and control of them. They also could hold positions where they could tell others what to do, like what to plant and when to harvest, but they could only hold those positions as long as the males of the tribe, who could neither own things nor tell anyone what to do, unanimously approved. This occurred during sometimes violent councils, though more often than not things worked themselves out peaceably and at worst the dissenters left the tribe.

This particular information about the Austrians I discovered in conversation with my host, whose name was Lotte, over a meal of goat stew and heavy grained bread. We sat on the floor of her circular hutch near a small fire; an opening above vented smoke, several pallets usable for beds or chairs lined the walls on which hung sagging skin bags, clothing, and simple objects I took to be weapons. When I asked her if life had improved since the growth of the bio-lens around the planet she did not respond for some time, but stood and walked away a few paces, turning her back to me.

"You work for them," she said.

"We all do, do we not?"

She turned to me again. "It's warmer, yet the dust storms are no better. There is rain in some regions, but it comes in giant storms. Chasms flood cataclysmically and then the water disappears. Many people have died. Like on earth, after they came."

"You mean Home? It happened before they came." Then I corrected myself. "Returned," I said.

"Who remembers?" she said. "You are homan, Marl. There must be something in you that understands us."

But it was not my decision whether or not to aqua-form Mars. Neither had I come to entertain disputes, old or new, over common knowledge, though I was surprised that our conversation had taken this turn. However intransigent the Indigos might be about preserving their ways, they seldom argued, much less intimated any desire for sympathy. Regardless, it was useless to say that the Austrians would not be flooded here on Olympus and that the other tribes could migrate south, a choice, it seems, few ever had on Home, whatever or whoever the cause of the world flood.

"I am only here concerning the fish," I said to Lotte.

She sat again and let her hood fall behind her head, revealing long flows of thick, black hair flicked with strands of silver. "There was a boy named Kurtz when I was young," she said. "A German. We weren't at war with the Germans at the time. He was a friend of my husband, Albert, though we were not yet married, only newly engaged. I was as young as the boy, barely ten."

"Nineteen," I said, "in Home years," for the years on Mars are twice as long.

"Yes. He fell in love with me. The friend. Kurtz. He was very sweet and very intense. But he came around often, too often, even when Albert was not here. It destroyed their friendship, and then Kurtz professed his love for me. I didn't love him, you see. Maybe I misled him, with kindness, with my attention, but I didn't love him. In time, wracked with heartache and pain, he apologized and left. We heard he'd gone south, to Newarabia or Newamerica. But within a year he returned, full of mystical stories: Africans who buried themselves beneath sand dunes, Brazilians who lived inside the bodies of snakes, Scandinavians inhabiting ice domes, cliff dwelling Australians, Laotians who hung in caves like bats, Chinese who lived on the backs of condors and who never touched the ground, and in the Marine Valley, the deadly Whites; jungles, magic, flying horses. He asked me to forgive him and I did. Then he left and that same night took his own life."

"So he is dead."

"For quite some time," she said. She took our bowls and placed them beside her. From under a pallet, a lean, quick moving animal emerged. It was black, almost blue, and about the size of my forearm.

It came to the bowl and Lotte stroked it before it began licking at the stew. Like all Nutian, we kept no domestic animals on Home. Keeping them was an ancient, wasteful habit, though here, these animals, called neocats, were used to clean up and kill pests. The animal made an odd, rumbling sound as it ate.

"I suppose Kurtz is not a common name," I said, though it was then that I saw something underneath the pallet, something pushed forward by the movement of the neocat, several sheets covered with scribbled marks. My eyes are good, but the light was not, though I had learned enough letters to be able to make out some of the largest ones on the top. It said, *Suffering*, and another word, *of*, *The Suffering of*, but that's all I could see. I would have asked her if I could see it, but Lotte had caught me gazing and did not offer. When I looked at her again she simple said, "It's memory."

"Memory," I repeated. "I encountered some of it on Gift Moon. A Pet-homan showed me some. She called it writing."

But my host now stared at me blankly, ungiving.

"Is there suffering here?" I said.

She stood again. "I hope you find your fish," she said.

XXXII

I hadn't much to go one, but by means of a few inquiries I found that there was a German living on the other edge of the village. He'd been captured years ago, as a child, during a raid on a German settlement and adopted after his parents were killed. His name was Auschenbach and he was now quite old, though he had a reputation, as more than one of the Austrians told me, "for keeping track of things."

I found him at home, sitting at a window in the heat of the magnified sun, smoking something, a shadow lying over him from the cross that split the square panes of glass, a shadow wavering in the gray of smoke and sunlight; I almost expected it to take shape and speak. The little house was filled with something I had not seen before, caged birds that cooed, fluttered, twittered and rattled in their wooden cages around him. When I entered he did not move to greet me, in fact he did not even stir. He spoke to the sunlight.

"It's as close as I can come to music, you know," he said.

To me, at the time, music was only a rumor. Aside from the chanting I'd heard among the cetaceans on Ghost Moon, I'd heard a kind of screaming and beating in the Wild Zones.

"I'm not very familiar with music," I said.

He turned to me and stood then. He was an older man, taller than me but darker and more squat than Lotte, though now, in the light, I noticed a touch of color on his cheeks. His hair was white and very thin, his face round. He dressed in loose fitting shirt and pants.

"Well, is one better off having known joy and lost it?" he asked.

"Are you Auschenbach?"

"Oh, questions is it?" he said. "Do you mean am I Auschenbach or am I better off?" He turned away and walked to the window again. "I'm not about to answer any questions if you're not here to share any news."

"News?" I said

"That's a question, unfortunately," he said.

"I was told that you keep track of things."

"I'm keeping track of you right now."

"You are German," I persisted.

He turned to me again. He drew on his smoke and exhaled. "You're speaking German," he said. "I barely noticed. Would you like a cigarette?"

I took one to be cordial and lit it with the end of his. We touched fingers then and he smirked. "At least you're warm-blooded," he said. "I'll join you." And he lit another cigarette of his own. We smoked for a while, there in his room, quietly, amid the skittering birds.

"So you're the fish man," he finally said, emitting smoke from his nostrils and mouth as he spoke. "We don't have much use for fish here."

"Not yet," I said.

He smoked again and exhaled. "That's a funny thing to say. I've always found Nutian rather humorless."

I almost denied that I was Nutian, but I caught myself. "I am not First-Nutian, as you can see."

"And when the Austrians find themselves living on a tropical island they won't need to smuggle fish," said Auschenbach.

"You might," I said, "at first. Maybe it was just practice."

"That would be foolish," he said.

He turned from me again and I took the opportunity to survey his cluttered hut. Each birdcage had a series of marks carved at the base, something I might previously have regarded as simply curious if not for my acquaintance with L.

"You write," I said.

He turned quickly, more quickly than he wished to show, though he recovered. It seemed I was not supposed to recognize writing. If this were true, then why not? And if not, then why had L been so eager to teach me? Indeed, maybe I was supposed to recognize it. Or was none of this connected at all?

"It's just scratchings," said Auschenbach. "Names."

"Kinds of birds?" I said. I walked toward the cages, glancing at the names etched into the wood. Some were scratched out with new markings set next to them.

He said, "No."

"Do you change them?" I asked. "The names? When the birds die?"

"Sometimes," he said.

"Sometimes? Why?" He was not being very forthcoming. I wanted to copy some of the names, but of course I had no instrument to do it, no tools. So many of them were completely unfamiliar, and whatever my intuitive skills at assimilating spoken language, writing seemed impenetrable and mysterious. There was a small bird named Alice, I recall, and another named Rabbit.

"Out of fondness," said Auschenbach, "and for memory."

"Memory," I said. "There are intui-cells."

"If we had Nutian technology, I'm sure the naming of birds would be suppressed as irrelevant by an intui-cell," Auschenbach said.

"Suppressed," I repeated.

"Censored."

Now we were getting somewhere. I was almost mumbling to myself, writing, irrelevant, revolution, fish. No, it fell apart. Then I encountered a name I recognized, carved into the bottom of an empty cage. *Kurtz.*

"Is this a common name, Kurtz?" I said to him.

"I don't think so."

"Lotte's friend, then. Her suitor, the boy who took his own life?"

"Kurtz?" he said. "Why no, I knew him well into middle-age. He had a daughter. But his wife died young."

"This cage is empty."

Auschenbach walked up and looked inside, tossing open the little door with his index finger, letting it swing. "You're trying to make something of a dead bird?" he said.

I turned to him then. "I am Marl," I said.

He took my hand. "I know," he said. "I am Gustave von Auschen-bach.

"Please tell me what you know about Kurtz."

Auschenbach turned. Unlike the Austrians he did not live around a central fire but kept a stone fireplace at the back of his hut. He had a table and chairs molded from the fiber of dead vines near the hearth and he gestured for me to sit, then joined me. He brought out two clay cups and poured a green-yellow wine, faintly carbonated and slightly sweet. But for the birds, the place was meticulous, the dirt floor swept to the smoothness of skin.

"Kurtz was somewhat below middle height, dark and smooth shaven, with a head that looked rather too large for his almost delicate figure," Auschenbach began.

XXXIII

"He wore his hair brushed back; it was thin at the parting, bushy and gray on the temples, framing a lofty, rugged, knotty brow—if one may so characterize it. His mouth was large, often lax, often suddenly narrow and tense; his cheeks lean and furrowed, his pronounced chin slightly cleft."

"You seem to have known him well," I said.

"He was well known," said Auschenbach. "He lived in the tribe of Munich and was a hero of the Seven Years' War against the Italians."

"A warrior," I said.

"No, a nurse. Later he was esteemed for his ideas."

"Famous for ideas?"

"The Germans are not like anyone else," Auschenbach said.

"Yet he is unknown on Home," I said.

"Are there ideas on Home?"

"What kind of ideas?" I persisted.

"Beauty."

"Maybe beauty," I said, "if not in that word. Work well done."

"Kurtz talked about it. He enjoyed controversy."

"Revolution," I said.

"Hardly," said Auschenbach. "He was a critic of other's ideas. He opposed war."

"We hardly need that idea on Home, where there is neither war nor the opposition to war," I said.

"We are back to the question of joy," he said. He went on for quite some time about ideas, though I understood little of it. Then he began again about Kurtz. "When he was older he was the first of the Germans to travel to the region of the Italian tribes. He left the Munichs and took up residence among the Venetians where he fell in love with a boy named Tadzio. The boy never knew. Kurtz first saw him one morning in the lounge of his hostel, his dark, curly hair falling onto his shoulders and his gray eyes like marbles and storms. After that Kurtz spent his days on the shore watching the boy fish, swim, bathe, play with his friends."

"What shore?" I said.

"The Hellas, where Venice floats like a dream."

It was a huge crater in the south, but I was unaware that it contained any water. How could I not know? "You say he fished. Here on Mars."

"I have never been there," Auschenbach said. "Kurtz became insane with the boy's beauty, so possessed that he felt mad and on several occasions tried to leave Venice, but each time returned more fitful and possessed. The boy seemed the embodiment of everything for which Kurtz had ever strived. Finally he decided to introduce himself, but looking in the mirror on the morning of his decision, he saw that he was just an old man, that to the boy, Tadzio, it would mean nothing. He fell into quiet, if desperate, resignation."

I sat at Gustave von Auschenbach's table, listening. I have tried to retell the story here, but in fact it took quite some time as Auschenbach went on and on with the details of Kurtz's passion and indulged in long descriptions of Tadzio as he stood in the sea, the water pinning his linen suit to his sculpted form; the glory of his rosy cheeks and flashing, gray eyes. It was as if Auschenbach himself had been there and revisited the memories a thousand times. At the window of the hut now, the sun had shifted and no longer cast its spray of fluttering light. It was early evening and hours had passed, yet Auschenbach went on.

"Then a plague struck Venice. Hundreds died, others evacuated, but as long as Tadzio stayed, so did Kurtz. One morning, feeling a little ill, he arose late and went to the docks where he watched families of evacuees board boats for crossing the Hellas Sea."

"The sea," I said. "Again you've mentioned a sea." But Auschenbach ignored me.

"Kurtz walked to the beach where his beauty, Tadzio—his parents packing and preparing to evacuate—played unsupervised. There Tadzio was fighting with a friend, another boy, who pinned him to the sand. Before Kurtz could rise to help, the other boy got up and walked away. They had been summer friends and the conquering child, over-come with remorse, tried to make peace, but Tadzio motioned him back with the jerk of one shoulder and went down to the water's edge.

"There he stayed a little, with bent head, tracing figures in the wet sand with one toe; then stepped into the shallow water, which at its deepest did not wet his knees; waded idly through it and reached the sand bar. Now he paused again, with his face turned seaward; and next began to move slowly leftwards along the narrow strip of sand the sea left bare. He paced there, divided by an expanse of water from the shore, from his mates by his moody pride; a remote and isolated figure, with floating locks, out there in sea and wind, against the misty inane."

Hours into the story now, it seemed we were talking more about the boy than Kurtz himself. I tried to interrupt my host, but he raised his hand.

"Once more the boy paused to look: with sudden recollection, or by an impulse, he turned from the waist up, and exquisite movement, one hand resting on his hip, and looked over his shoulder at the shore. Kurtz just sat just as he did that time in the hostel when first the twi-light gray eyes met his own. He rested his head against the chair-back and followed the movements of the figure out there, then lifted it, as it were an answer to Tadzio's gaze. It sank on his breast, his eyes looked out beneath their lids, while his whole face took on the relaxed and brooding expression of deep slumber. It seemed to him the pale and lovely Summoner out there smiled at him and beckoned; as though, with the hand he lifted from his hip, he pointed outward as he hovered on before into an immensity of richest expectation. And so, he rose to follow."

He sat quietly. Some minutes passed. "Auschenbach, the story of Kurtz," I finally said.

"That's all," he said. "Kurtz died."

"Dead? You say he followed. That he followed the boy into the sea."

"Yes. But what I meant was that he died."

"What you know of Kurtz is that he fell in love with a boy and died?'

"You asked."

"But you took such a long time."

"It's a long memory," he said.

"A story?" I asked.

He shrugged. "Poem. Story. The beauty," said Auschenbach. "What happens is almost irrelevant."

"You said there was a sea in the southern hemisphere," I said to him.

"Is there?" said Auschenbach.

I stood, irritated. Despite the changes on Mars, at night the cold closes like a fist. A chill swept the darkening room and I shivered. Auschenbach arose, stepped to the hearth and squatted by the fire, pushing it with a stick and blowing on it. It sprung to life and his hut broke into yellow light and fluttering sound, the shadows of the dangling cages dancing on the walls.

"You may sleep here," said Auschenbach. "By the fire would be best." There he offered a bed by dropping two, large, alpaca blankets. Despite their motley appearance, they were plush and warm and for the longest time I sat there quietly with him next to his fire as my heart settled in my chest under the physical silence of the settling birds. There was a richness here around me, an almost enviable thickness of life which I had never felt before. I felt satisfied, exhausted, cozy, and could not help but feeling that part of it was due to Auschenbach's quixotic tale.

Now I had two very different stories of Kurtz which agreed only in the assertion that he was dead. I had come to Mars searching for him and already I had encountered two rather complicated denials of his existence. Was it a tactic more devious than silence? Were they protecting him? Themselves? From me or from him? Yet if each story had led me circuitously to nothing, so too, each had led me to the next. Everyone who had mentioned him agreed on one thing, that he was either mythic or dead, which led me to induce that he was neither. I lay down that night determined to find my way to the Hellas Sea, and Tadzio.

XXXIV

In the morning Auschenbach served me a sweet cracker with green tea. I thanked him for the bed and food.

"I need a horse," I said to him.

"Maybe somewhere on the plains," he said.

"There are none here?"

"Have you seen any?" He eyed me cautiously as he sipped his tea.

I got up from the table and went to the cages, pretending to look at the birds, though I slowly made my way to the empty cage again. I studied the etching of Kurtz's name there below the door. It seemed then as if the *K* were the head and breast of a beast, the bottom right leg of the letter dropping slightly below the rest, like legs, and the *r* extending similarly below the base of the *u*; the *z* trailed off as if a tail, and the top right of the *K* flowed up and back like wings. I could not have been more convinced that the name on the cage was a picture, a beast, the same as I'd seen on L's medallion and Lotte's.

"I will walk then," I said to Auschenbach.

"Be safe," he said. "There are sometimes Austrian horse encampments at the base of the mountain, at the end of this trail, but if not you could find yourself quite alone."

"And if I find myself alone?"

"There are Italians on the plains, too, but we are at war with them."

"Italians. They're not on the Hellas?"

"Italians are everywhere, especially the horse Italians."

"I am not at war with them," I said.

"You might be," he said. "Is it true about the cetaceans on Europa?"

I was far too wizened to follow him. If he wished to implicate himself further that he knew of the unrest on Gift Moon, he would have to do it himself.

Auschenbach grinned, as if he'd succeeded in teasing me. "That they are speaking? German?"

"It seems you know as much as I do," I said. I thanked Auschenbach. He gave me bread and water for my journey and I left the village, accompanied at first by the tall, shadowy surfers who shifted around me on the black and silver boards and then, as I left the ledge, the dragonfliers who hovered above me, watching my way down the ravine. I was experienced enough and healthy enough to travel overland, though I could not help but wish I could master a dragonfly.

I accessed an intui-cell and knew the trail. I did not have much trepidation. I could survive, and if not I'd die.

XXXV

Soon enough I left the snow, and then the air was silent, too, and the sky unbroken but for the occasional dark-winged condors which swept the expanse above like aircraft, the swath of their wings so broad that they threw their smoky shadows over me like black gauze. The air thickened, as did the quiet, as if the planet itself held back a secret. I heard only the soft shuffle of my feet on the sandy path and sometimes the occasional skitter of lizards.

Olympus was an enormous yet gradual height and my descent took several days. At night I found shelter beneath ledges which shunned the wind but faced the rising sun. I set my heartbeat low and waited. Still, I was forced to ration my bread and water diligently and was glad to reach the plateau just above the broad red plain that swept from Olympus and stretched to the three volcanoes beyond. The Hellas Crater was almost half the planet and two seasons away, a long journey by any estimate, and I was exhausted and without provisions now, aside for the water my own body could provide by recycling. Yet in the distance, at what seemed the edge of an escarpment, I made out the intimations of activity: a yellow wall which stretched vaguely between a pair of redoubts, and some structures from which gray smoke swirled.

I struggled forward as what had appeared to be an hour's walk turned into two, and then three. The encampment, which originally appeared significant, seemed to shrink the closer I approached. In time I came to see that there was no fence across the valley, but only a wall of sand, no redoubts, but only two jagged rocks, rising above the desert like skeletal hands. There were no buildings, though it seemed once there had been people there, if briefly, with stones piled up here and there, apparently against the west wind.

I stared across barren Mars, here, a planet of dust, a thousand miles of desert to the southwest until the first plateaus of the southern hemisphere. Why not put it under water? Permit it to contribute? That aside, I could follow the base of the giant volcano westward in hope of finding some tribe encamped there under its protection. I had some time yet in the day. In most places, where life had taken hold, it filled niches everywhere. With patience it would let me see it.

Though the gravity of Mars makes it easy to move across the sand in great bounds, that could be as exhausting as running. I quickly learned to amble, or coast, across the sand. But things did not go well in terms of food or shelter. Around me, nothing stirred, and as I moved west the slope of the mountain grew more windswept and vulnerable. At the horizon the sun plummeted into dust, no, the ground rose up, airy, a brown sky flying, a sky turning to an advancing wall of dirt. The wind swept down the slope of Olympus carrying a vicious, nipping of sand. A Martian dust storm could tear an unprotected being's flesh from his limbs. It could last hours or weeks. I sat down, suddenly choiceless and numb. I felt the ghosts of a hundred other Nutian ambassadors lying there within their dried bones. I could not help but feel, as L might have said, the irony of my helpless fate, dying of starvation and thirst, battered to nothingness by the icy sand, waiting for my end on the bottom of a dry desert while I searched for a million stolen fish.

I thought I might climb back up the mountain, but I doubted I had the strength. What had I thought I'd find here? It seemed as if I had been tugged down the volcano by impulse, by absurdity, by intonation. How had I ever expected to wander here and find food and transportation? Had my wits been addled so? Who could live in this bitter place? In any regard, it mattered little. It became obvious why the Indigos offered so little resistance. There was little reason to take the life of a Nutian representative. They could simply offer up their world and let the wicked planet take the rest. As it was, I had failed no worse than those of purer blood.

Mars was yet a much colder planet than Home and soon the temperature dropped suddenly and precipitously; I gauged it at least one hundred degrees below freezing. I now judged the sandstorm to be but a few kilometers off. I lowered my mask and leapt up a short slope to a red boulder not much larger than me and dug a hole large enough in which to curl, and then, like a wild dog, spun in, rolling upon myself until covered by a layer of the Martian dirt. I lowered my heartbeat and temperature. With luck I'd awaken at the end, in a day or week or month, not buried too deeply to dig myself from a grave of sand.

XXXVI

"You think it's an egg?"

"It is buried. I would think if it were an egg, it would be buried."

"But because it's buried, that doesn't mean it's an egg."

"Nor, because it is an egg, does that mean it must be buried."

"A buried un-egg?'

"Maybe it is something that contains an egg."

"An egg container?"

"Well it wouldn't be the first time."

"It wouldn't? For whom?"

"I suppose for the egg itself."

"And for the container as well?"

"Well if it is always the first time for each egg and each container, how does it ever happen again?"

"How does it ever happen once, for that matter?"

"I am not an egg container," I said. I preferred to come out of hibernation more gradually, but the babble above had proved intolerable.

"I suppose it could be an eggless container," said the first voice.

"Everything certainly seems to contain something, wouldn't you say?" said the other.

"Listen," said the first voice, "I think it is a voice container."

"Fancy that," said the second.

I unraveled slowly to find myself beneath two, squat, round-bellied, almost neckless individuals with spindly arms and legs. They were standing next to the rock, each with an arm around the other's neck, and I knew which was which in a moment, because one of them had *DUM* embroidered on his collar and the other *DEE*. They wore short breast coats and high- waisted tight pants which flared out just above their thin ankles, though you could hardly call the center of either of them a waist. On their heads were caps with long, narrow bills.

They spoke so rapidly it was almost impossible to get a word in, and when I did they incorporated it immediately into their babbling.

"I am not a container of any sort," I said.

"Oh, I rather doubt that," said the first.

"Fancy you, hatching out of the desert floor and having any idea who you are."

"Do you think it's edible?"

"Oh, almost anything is edible," responded the second.

"Are we edible?" said the first.

"I'd rather well think we are."

"You'd rather well?"

"Well, rather."

"Who are you people?" I said.

"I know what you're thinking about," said Dum, the first, "but it isn't so nohow."

"Contrariwise," said Dee, "if it was so, it might be; but if it isn't, it ain't. That's logic."

"He'd like to know who we are," said Dum to Dee.

"Pops out of the sand, not even introducing himself, and he wants to know who we are," Dee said. "The first thing in a visit is to say 'How d'ye do?' and shake hands."

They released each other, bumped bellies and shook hands, then began dancing around in a ring. They chanted to each other, rather musically, like the dolphin ghosts, until they were both exhausted and stood panting. I had never before seen anything like them.

"Listen," I said, "I'm looking for someone named Kurtz."

"Kurtz," they said together, bumping bellies. "You'll have to speak to LS about that."

"Can you take me to him?"

"She's hardly a him," said the first twin. "And not being a him, then she's certainly not *him*. That's logic."

"And we haven't even had a proper introduction," said the second.

"I am Marl," I said. I managed finally to get to my feet. These were the first creatures on Mars I could actually look down upon.

""How d'ye do," they said together and paused together. "We are— goodness, who are we?"

"It's quite difficult, when you are so unique, to maintain one's references," the first said.

"Quite so," said the second.

"Check your collars," I suggested and they ignored me.

"Maybe LS will have some idea."

"Good idea," the second said and they headed up the embankment.

Still quite groggy and weak, I followed them and soon found myself at the mouth of a cave through which the two of them bounced like a pair of rubber balls. I hesitated, then began to follow, but they bounced back out. "First a story," they said together.

"Is it about Kurtz?" I said.

"You never know," said Dum. "How does one ever know quite what a story is about?"

"Do you like poetry?" said Dee.

"I'm afraid I don't know what that is."

The two of them hugged.

"Will it be very long?" I asked.

"Joy!" said Dum, "He wants a long one."

Well it was quite long and made very little sense, though the gist of the story was that a man and a walrus ate a bunch of oysters and for once, at least, Kurtz didn't die at the end. First Dum would speak, and then Dee, though everything that Dee said ended with the same sound with which he'd ended his last sentence. After a long while the oysters were eaten and wept over, then Dee wrapped up the tale and Dum said, "That's poetry."

If that was poetry, then it had been a dreadful story about dreadful, if verbally clever, creatures, but I told the twins that I enjoyed it and they seemed pleased. "May I see LS now," I said.

They bowed and bounced back into the cave and I followed. The interior was dusty, though luminous red. Light diffused and reflected remarkably off the stony walls from an opening above and behind a tall chair where sat sleeping an old woman, lanky and thin like other Indigos, though she wore a blue dress and white apron like a little girl's.

"LS?" I said.

"Sshh!" hissed the twins. "She's dreaming!"

"And what do you think she's dreaming about?" said Dum.

"How could I possibly know?" I said.

"About you!" said Dee. "And if she left off dreaming about you, where do you suppose you'd be?"

"Right here," I said.

"Wrong again," Dee said. "You're only a thing in her dream."

"When was I wrong the first time?"

"If she were to wake, we'd all go out like candles," said Dum.

"That's nonsense," I said.

"That's logic," they chimed.

"I'm willing to test that," I said.

"Please," said the old woman without opening her eyes. "Were I to awaken and you found yourself yet existing in front of me, you might likely believe that you existed and I was no longer asleep."

"I could as well be dreaming you," I said.

"Yes," she said, "of course."

My head began to ache. Never before had I felt such a longing to be out of someplace and be somewhere, anywhere, else, but most of all, Home.

"There," the old woman said, "now you feel just like Kurtz did." She raised her head and one eyelid lifted drowsily. In a moment, neither Dum nor Dee was there. She let her eyelid fall again.

"How did you do that?" I said.

She smiled.

"Are you LS?"

"Yes," she said.

"Were you ever a Pet?"

"I might have dreamt it once," she said thoughtfully.

"And Kurtz," I said.

"She came through a mirror and for the longest time couldn't find her way back."

"A dimensional portal?"

"A mirror."

"She?"

"A little girl."

"Kurtz is a little girl?" I said.

"We could have quite a time if you'd like to do all the things she did."

"Maybe another time," I said. "Right now I would simply like to find him."

"Her," she said.

"Her."

"I'm certain she's much older now," said LS. "Likely dead. The other side is rather ridged. One thing follows another, events appear to go only in one direction."

"You mean where she went back to," I said.

She raised her left hand and gestured, palm up, to the wall. "The mirror is right here," she said.

And so it was, however I had failed to notice it before. It was not like our mirrors now, though Nutian have little use for them, that is, not a reflective lens like an eye, but something solid and hard and bright and it stood in a brown, wooden frame. There, within, I saw myself, and an empty chair where I thought LS sat, though when I turned back to her, there she was, asleep. In the mirror again, the chair disappeared and I saw myself sleeping in the sand beneath the rock where I'd first met Dee and Dum. I stepped toward it and in a moment I was again beneath the red boulder, out in the sand.

Though I did not remember waking up, I was standing, as perfectly awake as I'd been in the cave only moments before. I gathered myself and walked away from the hill. I did not want to find the cave and I most certainly didn't want to run into those horrible twins. And my plight was now worse than when the sandstorm originally arose. I checked the sun. It had passed from late winter to spring. I had been unconscious for over a month. I was weak, had no food and no water but what I could recycle on my own. I knew of no one and nowhere I could go to for help.

The red desert stretched out under the pink, Martian sky, lifeless and dry but for the arousal of dust on the horizon, likely another dust storm under which, this time, I might sleep myself into never-ending bliss. I nonetheless supposed myself fortunate that besieged as I was by doom and calamity I could not think too clearly about LS, Dee, Dum, and the little girl named Kurtz who came to Mars through an old mirror. Something in the universe, my universe anyway, had changed beneath my feet.

XXXVII

I trudged southward and west, obliquely toward the horizon and the storm. It mattered little. Good things end, bad things come, good things come again, and then again the bad. In fact, I began chanting this to myself, making, for the first time in my life, my own music; singing. How absurd. I would have to raise this issue of music with the Nutian. Even more absurd. I imagined myself standing before them, humming away while being led off to a Wild Zone. The dust rose in the west, though I noticed it was no longer a wall of dust, but a circle, and as it approached I made out individual clouds, and then riders. I stopped and watched as they came down upon me, riding their tall, graceful, red beasts that flew over the sand in great bounds, several of the riders holding poles from which whipped banners of green, white, and red.

The riders on the backs of these animals must have stood almost four meters high, their banners extending another meter into the air. There were about twenty of them and they circled several times, the ground becoming a rumble under the animals' hooves. As they collapsed their circle I noticed that there were as many females among them as males, for they all went naked, despite the chill, each of them painted idiosyncratically in the same colors as their flags. They halted, surrounding me, all of them gorgeous and young, none more than twelve Martian years, each of them wearing their dark hair long upon their shoulders; brooding brows, thick, pouting lips. Their horses wore blankets from which hung water bags, food pouches, and what I recognized as weapons, lances, bows and arrows. They and their beasts heaved in front of me, the breasts of the young women rising and falling with supple softness on their chests. Since my encounter with L, I found their youth and nudity distracting.

"I am Marl," I signed, "an ambassador from Home." When no one answered I signed it again, turning as I did so all of them could see.

Finally one of the women whispered to the lad next to her who signed back to me, "We could care less."

"I would appreciate some help," I said.

They all laughed. I felt a thump on the back of my neck and when I awoke I was being carried on the back of a horse like a sack, my feet and hands bound, my head on one side of the horses flank and my feet on the other. The tail of the beast whipped my face raw, as did the wind. I discovered, as well, that horses fart all of the time, a foul stench if at least a warm one. This is how I spent the next several days, at night thrown to the edge of the fire circle, raw and sore, to fend for myself, which was not very well since I was left bound. When they were done eating and drinking—something which I found encouraging because they had neither hunted nor foraged, so must have been, I assumed, between storage centers or settlements—a piece of something salty and chewy was thrown on the ground near my face, and later I was given a sip of wine.

In fact most of their pouches were filled with wine, not water. They carried very little water, camping at dusk near hidden waterholes from which they refreshed their horses. Near these waterholes there was usually enough greenery for the horses to forage, though each rider carried grain sacks, too. They recovered their horses' fecal matter as they moved along, dried it, and used it to fuel fire at night, around which they sat wrapped in the same blankets which they placed on their horses' backs during the day. They drank wine constantly and each time before drinking raised their cups in the air to each other, even on horseback, even at a run. In the morning they ate almost nothing, but drank a black, bitter liquid that made their dark eyes dilate and fill with fire. They called it *café*. Though they paired off each night when they retired, everyone seemed to have sex with everyone else and they seemed to do it morning, noon, and night, when they were getting along and when they were not, under the moons, under the sun, on the backs of their horses.

They did not seem curious about me at all, taking interest in nothing about me, not even, thank the Void, in my leathers, in which I'd actually been able to build up a reservoir of water. In a weeks time my stomach muscles had adjusted to my riding position and my exposed skin hardened. Then, after a few more days of listening to them, I began to pick up their language—Italian. Indeed, I had plenty of time to practice to myself. I understood now, from overhearing, that supplies were low and they would soon have to come to some decision about finding a friendly settlement or raiding a less friendly one or, if they must, raiding a friendly one; they seemed to be at war with everybody, though some more than others, and yet while constantly professing to each other that they were afraid of no one, they seemed less anxious to encounter some groups. Like the Germans. They despised Germans and if I had spoken it to them upon our encounter I would likely have been murdered on the spot.

It seemed we were traveling upon a sort of vaguely defined alleyway of war upon which, come later spring and summer, great edible beasts migrated north and south, following the seasons to graze on the weeds which grew in a swathe along this corridor that swept southwest down to the city of Firenzi, northeast of the Hellas and Venizia, my destination. However many tribes made their settlements alongside this path, the Italians, by means of these youthful, roving, hunting and warring parties, made life very uncomfortable for everyone else and they were quite proud of it, too. Amid all of this, they didn't really seem to have anyone who was in charge. Among my feeders and handlers, some seemed to treat me with less belligerence, if not more sympathy, a female in particular, not one of the leaders, for she was quite young, but the one who whispered into the ear of the young man I spoke to at the time of my capture. One night, after they'd fed and drank, played and sung themselves toward their inevitable heroic speeches, I spoke to the young woman, the whisperer, upon whose horse I'd spent the day and who that night owed me the ration of her choice. In the past she'd been more generous than others. *"Grazi,"* I said, and she answered *"Prego,"* unthinking, then turned to walk away before pausing in her tracks and turning to me. The light of both Mars' quick little moons flew in the sky and threw the shadows of cactuses around us like spots. In the moonlight I made out her face, pouting and quizzical under her thick, dark hair that fell upon her blanketed shoulders and down to her naked breasts. In the distance, something howled.

I struggled, finally sitting up. She watched.

"You are powerful," I said to her, for I'd picked up some of the etiquette of intercourse, "and I am gracious."

"If you think I am soft, you are mistaken," she said.

"I do not."

"Why have you chosen silence until now?"

"What would I have done? Beg for my life? Boast? Pretend false friendship?"

"Boasting would have been best," she said. "Of those three." Her eyes roved over me suspiciously, scanning my bonds to make sure I was not springing a surprise.

"I shall remember that," I said.

"Intelligent prisoners generally isolate their weakest opponent," my guard said, then she stepped closer and sat, her feet perched flatly beneath her and her behind floating inches from the ground, solidly balanced yet lithe, like a predator.

"In truth, it has taken me this long to learn your language."

"You just learned it," she said. She opened her blanket and revealed, among other things, a narrow belt on her waist, from which dangled a knife on her left hip and two curved, conical cups on her right. The ubiquitous wine skin hung from her shoulder, the strap crossing her painted chest between her breasts.

"By listening," I said.

"But you didn't learn it just this minute. You learned it over time and chose to speak it now."

"You are a wisdom holder," I said to her. "Others consult your opinion. And of the most generous of people, you have been the most generous to me."

"You've learned more than our language," said my host. "What other languages do you speak?"

This was one very intelligent primitive. "This, the sign language," I signed, then said, "Nutian and Homan."

She took the cups from her belt and holding them in one hand by their narrow bottoms squeezed wine into both, wedging them upright on a rock in front of her. "You came from space," she said. "We found you southeast of Olympus. So you spent time with the mountain Austrians. I assume you expected supplies at the foot of the mountain but found their camp rubbed out."

"It's true. I passed through the Austrian settlement on Olympus. But I am not partisan," I said.

"Maybe you should be."

"Is it too late?" I offered a slight grin.

"Yes, of course it is," she laughed.

So I took the opportunity to explain my mission, my trip to Europa, as the Indigos called the moon, and my search for Kurtz.

"So you speak German," she said when I was done. "You lied."

"An omission," I said.

"It was a smart lie," she said. She took her knife from her belt and stood over me, brought the blade down and traced my hairline on my forehead. She licked it. I felt my blood drip into my eyes, then tasted it at the corners of my mouth. Then she sliced downward quickly, but all she did was cut the twine at my wrists. My hands were free.

"You are not Nutian. You have our blood," she said and handed me the cup. We toasted. "To Italian, the mother of Languages."

"I learned German on Europa," I said to her. "From the whales."

She laughed and poured again. "For that story you earn another toast," she said.

"It's true."

We drank again. "Anything else you say tonight will be disregarded," she said, then cut the twine from my feet. "I am Beatrice. Come, join us."

XXXVIII

I followed her to the circle of drinking braves who accepted my presence with barely a nod. She opened her arms and yelled, "We are the Young Italians!" which created a great burst of yelping and dancing around the flames. After they settled down, Beatrice reintroduced me and began to tell them why I had come, but they laughed and laughed, interrupting her with toasts and hoots. They patted me on the back and encouraged me to tell them my story myself, which I did, between a hundred interruptions of laughter and toasts. In particular, the part about the German speaking Orcas drove them mad with glee.

When I was done they toasted again and Beatrice shouted, "He wants to hear the story of Kurtz!" After much cheering a brave named Dante who appeared to be the oldest and shortest of them, barely two heads taller than me, stood. The band quieted and in a wavering, almost singing voice, yet in a manner much like Dum and Dee, though in this case making matching sounds at the end of every first and third line, told the story of a young man named Kurtz who is led by the ghost of his dead lover to a place called Hell, one of the realms these Young Italians believed that they went to after they died, a place full of demonic creatures who inflict horrible tortures upon the dead. It was a very long story full of unspeakable descriptions of pain that got worse and worse the farther down into Hell Kurtz traveled.

Dead people, or shadows as Dante called them, live on after death, headless, dismembered, buried in fire, in ice, in shit. Some are bodiless faces buried in rock where demons come by to sit on their open screaming mouths and defecate in them.

After a while a new ghost named Virgil takes over as Kurtz's guide and around the bonfire a new story-teller named Virgil took up where Dante left off. Kurtz goes down and down into the icy and fiery depths of Hell and on the way down he meets friend and foe alike, people he once found noble as well as enemies he once thought bad. Hell is an eternal place and the lost souls must stay there eternally. I was certain this implied that the story must go on eternally, too, but finally, at the center of Hell, Kurtz encounters a horrible, winged beast with heads in his armpits. Each of the heads eats people, though they never die; they are eaten and regurgitated and eaten again and again. "The horror," Kurtz mutters as the creature reaches for him. "The horror."

The story lasted until almost dawn, though at the end Kurtz does not get eaten by the beast, but escapes and emerges back on the surface of Mars under a sky of stars.

"He doesn't die?" I asked.

"Not yet," said Beatrice. "There are two more."

Around me the Young Italians began to couple off and make for sleep around the fire.

"You're free to do what you want," Beatrice said to me. "You're my responsibility now."

"Free?" I said. "I could take one of your horses."

"Good luck," she said.

"And if I succeed?"

"I will be tortured in place of you."

"And if I stay?"

"You will be tortured when we reach Firenzi."

"For what purpose?" I asked.

"To kill you, of course," she said. "Though if you remain absolutely silent and survive, recovering in able health, you might be adopted."

In one moment both set free and given a death sentence, I was too perplexed to speak.

Beatrice put her hand on my shoulder. "There is really no way to know the truth of anything you've told us. Whatever your intentions, the simplest thing is to end your life. It would dishonor you to let you live long enough for us to find out you have lied to us or could harm us."

"I won't harm you."

"Certainly not," she laughed. "But you could pass information about us to others."

"We've toasted and told stories," I said.

"I hope that will continue," she said. "We like you. But it is very simple. You are not one of us, so we'll kill you." She took her hand from my shoulder and wrapped her blanket around her chest, then turned away from me, looking up to the stars. "Would you like some advice?" she said.

"Of course."

"If you boast in Italian, they will kill you more quickly."

"You are very gracious, Beatrice," I said.

"Thank you," Beatrice said.

XXXIX

Now in Beatrice's charge, I spent my days riding double behind her as we sped westward across the Amazon Plain, the land around us growing more green as we flew. We drank and told stories each night, though the most popular by far was my tale of the German speaking whales on Europa, which threw my executioner/hosts into great fits of laughter. Near the equator we encountered our first of the migratory *bufalo*, enormous beasts that looked like small hills in the distance. The mounted Young Italians broke upon them, separated a cow, and the big warrior Aeneus took her down with an arrow between the head and withers, then a lance thrust guided perfectly to the heart through the opening between her ribs. That night we ate richly and I shared the heart of the beast with them. The engorged organ was barely seared over the flames and burst with thick, murky tasting blood as soon as one sunk one's teeth into it. We sat, slurping wine, our chests and faces sopping with blood.

The dried *bufalo* feces helped make a tremendous fire and that night Dante and Virgil told the second part of the Young Italian poem. Kurtz visits another afterlife realm called Purgatory. The souls or shadows suffer unspeakable tortures there, as well, but in this story there are long speeches and debates about whether or not anybody is going to get out. This seemed pertinent to the Young Italians because somehow or another this was the place where most of them believed they were going to end up. Every so often a new brave would stand and toast the storyteller, then take over where the last left off, a pack of young, drunk ruffians, gnawing raw *bufalo,* blood dripping from their necks and shoulders, reciting poetry. Thus they debated, in verse, some nonsensical relationship between torture and transgression.

Before the end, my guardian, Beatrice, stood and recounted how Kurtz once again met his dead lover, also named Beatrice, who led him out of Purgatory, back to the surface of Mars under a starry sky. The tribe rose as one and cheered, "Bravo! Bravo!" lifting their cups which I now recognized as hollow *bufalo* horns. In time, they lay down, bulging bellies skyward.

"Beatrice," I said to my guardian, "what does it mean?"

"It means what it means," she said.

"Do you believe all of that?"

"Believe?" she said.

"Who is Kurtz?" I said.

"You know better than I. You are looking for him. Who are you looking for?"

"Is he alive?" I asked.

"He is the founder of Italy. He traveled here, to Mars, after his city was conquered by the Nutian, fighting and outwitting many monsters, experiencing many adventures. These trips to the Afterlife are only part of all he did."

"He's very old?"

She tilted her gorgeous head at me, touched my cheek with her rough hand. "Marl, you are too little for us."

"Beatrice," I said, "why does everyone have the same names as the people in the story?"

"Why does somebody who's going to die so soon want to know so much? Wait for the end," she said.

The Young Italians did not waste any part of the *bufalo* and spent the following morning roasting and drying meat, readying the skin to cure on racks which they mounted on the backs of their horses; they sucked the marrow from the bones then fashioned them into tools: mallets, hatchets, sewing needles, knives. They also saved sacks of fat which they claimed in Firenzi they could solidify and mold over wicks for fire. From the bladder they made a kind of ball, which they batted about, keeping it constantly in the air as they rode.

Off again, they had apparently accomplished their war mission before my capture and were now flying for home. Encountering the *bufalo* herd had been fortuitous in that we didn't need to raid any settlements for provisions, but we were running out of wine and the push to reach Firenzi became urgent. They argued among themselves whether to take a longer, safer route along the equator, across a Plain they called Elysium, or to drive southward onto the plateau region through a pass guarded by a German city named Munchen.

I spoke freely among them because, well, why not? "You'd rather risk your lives than run out of wine," I said.

"Maybe we could find your fish freighter," said Aeneus, "and the German whales could negotiate safe passage for us." He was the tallest and strongest of them, the one who first spoke to me at my capture and the one who killed the *bufalo*. He often slept with Beatrice.

"You are the Young Italians, the greatest horsemen on Mars. You can't ride by a German town?"

"What do you know of it?" Aeneus said.

Beatrice spoke to me. "The Germans are cruel barbarians."

"They drink beer and Reisling," Virgil said.

"White wine," Beatrice informed me. "Not red."

"Let me speak to them for you. They are homan like you and I."

"We are the human beings," said Aeneus. "They are Martian barbarians who have forgotten."

"Forgotten? Do you mean they have no memory? No poems?"

"You are of the Nutian," Dante said to me. "The Nutian have outlawed memory."

"The Nutian have no laws and no outlaws," I said.

"Marl, the Germans have *machinas*," Beatrice said.

It was the first time I'd heard any version of the word *machine* in a very long time. I knew they were things that were used on Home before the Return, things that caused the ecological degeneration of Home. I knew, as well, that the Indigos and Nutian long shared a compatibility in the rejection of them, a sympathy which the two cultures seemed to nurture for a long time, though the implications of aqua-forming the northern hemisphere of Mars had changed that.

"All the better reason you let me go to them," I said.

"You'd simply stay with them and we wouldn't get to kill you," said Aeneus.

"Why stay with them? They wouldn't take me to Venezia."

"With us, you will not get any closer than Firenzi."

"I am here to find out about the fish freighter and to make peace," I said.

"*La Gloria di colui che tutu move per l'universo penetra e risplende in una parte piu e meno altrove*," sang out Dante. It was the beginning of a very, very long night.

XL

Outside the walls of Munchen, perched on a tall, Martian mare, I held a pole with a white flag. I'd had little sleep and too much wine. Running low on wine didn't change anything for the Young Italians. I haven't mentioned before how they accompanied their singing, but they beat upon logs with sticks, hooted through reeds in which they'd made holes with bone drills, made sounds with strings stretched over bones and gourds. Beatrice leading, they sang all night, a very confusing diatribe about a god who was three people.

All of the planets were mentioned and they seemed at once both gods as well as planets, though you could not stay in Paradise if you believed that, and then there were stories told from a thousand other mystical beings called saints and angels. Mostly what people did in Paradise was launch hateful invectives toward the inhabitants of earth, particularly those in charge of leading souls to paradise, and more particularly, Italians. I could understand how Kurtz was quite confused by it all and lucky for him he didn't have to stay there in Paradise. Nonetheless, there were plenty of times that Jupiter, as well as Europa and Mars, were mentioned and I took this as good sign that I was on the right track.

Dante spent the night next to me, whispering in my ear, explaining how one of the three gods, Christo, had a huge battle up in Paradise with and angel named Diablo who lost and now ran Hell. That was the beginning of the whole mess, war in particular, I supposed. Later Christo, born of a homan virgin, appeared on Home and got killed by the ancient Italians. In fact, they tortured him. I assumed, at first, that that's why they all felt so bad about their prospects for Paradise but, in fact, they declared the opposite. Guilt just led to more of the same bad behavior that caused it, which fairly well explained the depth, beauty and cruelty of these Young Italians: blood is wine, virgins give birth, murder saves you.

But at the end of this *Paradiso* everyone is singing quite happily, much as the Young Italians did around their campfire, full of great love and rejoicing because all beings, though especially the Young Italians, were the Father God's children, mothers aside. The Young Italians fell upon each other in an orgy of affection, during which Aeneus took the time to gather a mare and pack me off to treat with the Germans, guessing, I supposed, that I'd been so transformed by their great poem that my loyalty went unquestioned, despite my impending execution. It was all rather interesting in an undisciplined sort of way.

I waited quietly outside the gates of Munchen, which I'd come to understand was the same city as the Munich to which Auschenbach referred. If the Munchens had heard of Kurtz, I might make another connection. The high walls of the town buzzed above me with shouts and clambering. Finally the gates opened and a dozen horsemen emerged in a line riding thick, white beasts. Unlike the Young Italians they were fully dressed, men as well as horses, every other one in dark red or dark green and I could see, as well, that they wore a kind of plating or hard covering, particularly over their heads and chests. They moved in absolute, rigid unison, as methodical as sunset, until they stopped before me and one of them, dressed in dark red, pranced his steed forward.

I spoke in German. "I am Marl of the Home Nutian," I said.

"On a Roamin mare?" he said.

"Roamin?" I asked.

"The Italians who roam. The scum and scourge."

"We are all Nutian," I said. "All homan." Now I could make out his blue eyes and light brows. Unlike the ragged Italians horses, the white beasts before me stood rigidly, their heads bent forward at their armored necks, steam rolling from their nostrils into the thin air. "May I treat with you?"

"You speak German. We can talk. But out here. Not in the city."

He motioned with his hand and the green riders departed for the gates. When they opened this time I heard pounding and rumbling. I noticed, as well, that the creatures which hovered and dove in the sky above the city walls were not creatures at all, but nine long-haired homans mounted inside frail structures with outstretched, translucent wings. For the first time now I felt a hot surge in the wind, almost like breath, yet unnatural, a kind of rigid heaving that matched the pulse of the rumbling within the town. The sky beings rose and dove on that pulse.

Further, what I had taken to be storm clouds beyond the walls I now saw to be smoke, arising from within the city itself.

My host, watching my eyes, said, "The Valkarie," but of course it meant nothing to me.

"You're making clouds?" I said.

The green riders returned with a tarp and poles, among other things, and with their compatriots erected a tent. My host removed his headgear. He had a sweep of blond hair that fell over his right eyebrow though the rest of his hair was cropped short above his ears. He leapt from his steed in a single bound while two red riders helped me dismount. Inside the tent some pillows lay beside a low table. On the table stood two tall, clear containers filled with an amber, bubbling liquid topped with white froth.

"I am Captain Peter von Sievers," my host said.

"I am traveling with the Young Italians," I said. When he did not respond I said, "The Roamin," and he nodded.

"Is it true they fuck their horses and sleep with them?" Peter von Sievers said.

"They are certainly capable of fucking *on* their horses," I said.

Von Sievers raised his glass and I mimicked him. We nodded to each other. I assumed we were drinking the dreaded German beer. It was slightly bitter, but aromatic. Were I a Pet, it would have spoken to me of aggressive and confident precision.

"The Roamin are barbarians," von Sievers said to me. "Why are you traveling with them?"

I supposed it would have been no news to him that the Young Italians felt equal aversion for the Germans. "I came down from

Olympus—" I started, but von Sievers frowned so completely that I adjusted. "From the Austrians."

"From Valhalla," Peter von Sievers said. "And the Nibelung."

"They called themselves Austrians."

"They have been confused for a while," he said.

"I failed to find their village at the base of the mountain and became lost in the desert. The Roamin found me. They are taking me to Firenzi."

"For public torture?"

"I'm going to Venizia where I hope to find out something about Kurtz."

"Are you so brave and wily?" said Peter von Sievers. He brushed his hair from his brow with a flick. "But you will find nothing in Venizia about Kurtz."

"The Austrians seemed to think he'd been there," I said and drank some more of the beer. "And that he was from here."

"What little the Nibelung know of Kurtz, they learned from us, Herr Marl."

"Marl is fine," I said.

"What about the aqua-forming?" said von Sievers.

"You live in the mountains on plateaus," I said.

"Where will everyone else go?"

"I've passed through kilometers of nothing," I said.

Von Sievers placed his beer in front of him. "I resent the implication, Herr Marl. You are here because of the missing fish freighter. Everyone on Mars knows this, so why must you be so equivocal?" Now, as he spoke, he waved his hands around his mug in quick, expressive jerks. "How would we hijack a space freighter? Where would we put it? And why not wait for the Nutian who will bring their own fish in due time?"

"Aqua-forming would create more rivalry," I said to him. "If I can be so direct, I thought everybody here liked war."

Von Sievers stood and then paced. He paused and stared at the bare tent wall. The red glow of sunlight, reflecting from the crimson rocks, danced on the skin of the structure which moved in the breeze as if breathing. But it was not breathing. It was made of a material that, if organic, was certainly dead. I thought of these Germans then behind their walls of dead stone and the things behind those walls. Unimaginable things.

"You're wearing something on your hip," I said. "You've made no attempt to hide it."

Von Sievers turned and withdrew a long, glittering object that came to a point. It was thin and shiny, rather like a long, stiff, fish. But it had a handle and had been engraved with a figure I'd come to recognize. A dragon, a figure which was becoming as ubiquitous and mysterious as Kurtz himself.

"Is that a weapon?" I asked.

He arched an eyebrow. "A sword."

"Who would you use that on?" I asked.

"Anyone?" he said.

"Anyone? Nutian?"

"I will tell you what I know about Kurtzfried," he said.

"Kurtz," I said. "Yes?"

He put up his hand. "He is German," said von Sievers.

"No doubt," I said.

He raised his sword and began to sing. As he began, other Germans entered the tent and sang as well, in voices low and thunderous, they each raised their swords above their foreheads. They sang. They drank beer. They sang. To Kurtzfried, the greatest warrior of all.

XLI

Like the Young Italians, each of these Germans took his turn, though soon women had joined us as well and I could discern that each person before me had assumed a part of the story, at times actually repeating the action of the person they sang about. Kurtzfried, it seemed, was the child of unwitting incest. His parents, Kurtzmund and Kurtzlinde, twins, were separated as children when Kurtzlinde was kidnapped during a battle. Their father, slain in the raid, had been the last Indigo who knew how to forge steel.

"Like your weapons," I said, but they ignored me and sang on.

Before the Steelfather died, he engraved the memory of how to forge steel onto a golden ring.

"Writing," I said.

"Quiet," said von Sievers.

The Steelfather left Kurtzmund under the protection of a great king and queen, Wotan and Fricka., who lived on Vallahalla, where the Nibelung now resided. The Steelfather gave Wotan his son, the ring, and his sword to be passed on to Kurtzmund at manhood. Wotan and Fricka had nine daughters. The first Valkyrie. So Kurtzmund, an only son, was dear to them.

But only Byrnhilde, the oldest of the Valkyrie could understand the ring's memory. Regardless, the ring was stolen by an Italian who had little understanding of the object's value. When Wotan went to retrieve it, the battle was interrupted by a beast, a dragon, who breathed fire and melted all the swords. She took the ring and swept the planet of steel weaponry. But for the one sword given to Wotan by the Steelfather.

"Of course," I said. I pointed at von Siever's sword.

"You will have to stop interrupting," whispered von Sievers.

In honesty, there was a legend on Home, an irrational story, that a beast put an end to the Age of Machines, but not in time to stop global warming. It explained, for homans who needed an explanation for the demise of their dominance, how the passive Nutian overcame, or saved, I'd begun to understand that it depended on your perspective, the planet so easily.

Regardless, the Niebelung dragon had a mate and while the dragon queen patrolled the planet, sweeping it of weapons and the means of making them, the male took the ring to his cave. All that was left of weaponry and steel was the last sword, given to Kurtzmund by Wotan when Kurtzmund reached manhood.

"This is quite a poem," I said.

"It is history," said von Sievers. "The Nutian have denied us history."

And for good reason, I thought.

"The man who had stolen Kurtzlinde, named Alberich, was a Nibelung and Kurtzmund came upon him in his first travels to the three great mountains across from Vallahalla. As Alberich hosted Kurtzmund to a great meal, he plotted to steal the last sword from him, failing to notice that his own wife, Kurtzlinde, was falling in love with Kurtzmund. At the same time, Byrnhilde, the princess of the Valkyries, fearing for this precise event, planned to fly to Alberich's to intercede, but Wotan, bitter and tired of conflict, made her pledge not to interfere.

Disobeying her father, Byrnhilde flew to Alberich's land, only to find that Kurtzlinde and Kurtzmund, brother and sister, had fled and consummated their love. Alberich followed them and murdered Kurtzmund in his sleep. With the rock he used to murder Kurtzmund he also broke the last sword. Enraged, Byrnhilde slew Alberich with the broken sword and returned to Wotan with Kurtzlinde and the broken weapon. Wotan imprisoned his daughter in a ring of fire for breaking her promise to him. Kurtzlinde died giving birth to Kurtzfried.

Here, everyone cheered and toasted and drank beer. "This is complicated," I said, though I had to hand it to them, for all its convolutions it seemed an attempt to get to the bottom of something.

"The world is complicated, Herr Marl," said von Sievers. "More complicated than words, which are frail and simple." He raised his glass. "To Kurtzfried!" he said.

I'd failed to notice it until then, but now I saw the shadows of yet more Germans gathered around the tent. I could feel them, I could smell them, listening. We toasted again.

"So we have come to the Kurtz," I said.

And they once again began to sing. Kurtzfried grew up a powerful man, so powerful that in his prime he was strong enough to defy Wotan, who like everyone else had become afraid of the dragons and given up all thought of weapons and the means to make them.

"Machines," I said.

Von Sievers put a finger to his lips and then wagged it at me.

Kurtzfried sneaked to the dragon cave and stole the ring. He freed Byrnhilde from Wotan's fire ring and the two of them, using the instructions on the ring, repaired the last sword. When the dragon emerged from his cave to retake the ring, Kurtzfried slew him. Fearing Kurtzfried, the dragon queen retired to the cave and Kurtzfried and Byrnhilde fell in love.

There was again great toasting and cheering.

"You may speak now," said von Sievers.

"So you Germans here in Munchen, the children of Kurtzfried and Byrnhilde, possess the sword and the technology to make more." I was delighted. Not only was there a happy ending for a change, I was proud of my ability to infer the end of these infernal poems. "You are all descendents of Kurtzfried!" I said to my host.

"I am Captain Peter von Sievers, Herr Marl," said von Sievers. "Kurtzfried eclipsed even Wotan in power and eminence. He shared the knowledge of the sword with all the Germans and all the Nibelung. Yet Alberich's son, Gunther, plotted revenge against Kurtzfried and Byrnhilde."

And once again the singing began. Gunther invited the couple to his land, to reconcile and celebrate their engagement, but then gave Kurtzfried a potion by which he forgot Byrnhilde and fell in love with

Gunther's sister. Byrnhilde fell into despair. Then, while together on a hunt, Gunther put a sword in Kurtzfreid's back and murdered him. At the moment of death Kurtzfried remembered Byrnhilde who came to his side. Kurtzfied died in disgrace and shame.

"Disgrace and shame?" I said.

"Quiet, Herr Marl."

Byrnhilde, hopeless, took her own life with her husband's sacred sword.

"By the Nutian!"

"Herr Marl," said von Sievers, "there followed many long battles, both noble and bitter, between the Germans and the Nibelung on the slopes of Vallahalla. That is yet another history. But after long months of bitter war, no one survived."

"No one survived?" I said. "That's impossible! Why didn't you end the story where I ended it?"

Von Sievers looked at me quizzically. "I told it as it is told," he said. "What would be accomplished by a poem in which people go on to live happily? I have witnessed many sad deaths, many heroic deaths, noble ones, pathetic ones, but never anyone who lived forever happily."

"How could no one survive?" I pressed him. "Who lived to tell the story? Who passed on the knowledge of weapon making?"

"The story did," von Sievers said.

"Who told you the story?"

"Stories tell people. People do not tell stories," said my host. "First the explanation, then the fact. Explanations that come after the fact are fantasies, and usually very self-serving ones, wouldn't you agree?" Von Sievers began petting his sword again with his gloved hand. "Would you have us believe that from war, the most horrible thing, emerged fast marriage, productivity, bliss?"

"I would have you believe that war is an anachronism, unknown to the Nutian and long ago abandoned on Home."

He laughed. "Maybe someday we shall bring you back to your senses. Now, would you like us to save you from the idiotic Italians?" he said.

"I am here to negotiate passage for the Italians."

"Who will torture and kill you."

"I hope they will be in my debt."

"They will torture you longer in honor of their debt."

"They've promised me a quick death if I insult them in Italian," I said.

Von Sievers laughed hard and drank. He called in the Germans from outside the tent who congratulated their comrades on a well told poem. I had my knuckles crushed in many hard handshakes. Suddenly there seemed to be beer everywhere. They clinked their mugs above their heads, roared, and chanted together, a poem about throwing corpses from a hall, all ending in sorrow, as joy must ever turn to sorrow in the end. Deep into the cold, Martian night, these Germans drank and sang until at the hour of false dawn I approached von Sievers again.

"These Italians drink and sing just like you. I have been with them for a long time. I am the Nutian ambassador and I must to get to Venizia."

"They're murderous blood drinkers who fuck horses," he said, his brow sinking over his eyes.

"If you let us pass, when I return Home I will have forgotten about your machines."

"You will be dead anyways," he said.

"Then better by their hands then yours, no?"

"You are implying reprisal?" snorted von Sievers.

"Only moral culpability," I said, "for my inevitable death."

He smiled broadly. These Germans were going to be trouble, even if the Nutian succeeded in aqua-forming the north; they would be here on the plateaus with their dragon swords of sorrow and joy, their Valkyrie, their machines, their duty, their morbid heroism. I did not trust them and preferred the wild Italians who were threatening to torture me to death.

Von Sievers turned his back to me, yet continued speaking, almost too softly to hear. "A band of about twenty?" he said.

"Yes."

"Men and women."

"Yes, of course."

He waited for a while before he spoke again. "If they will ride by us openly, in daylight, beneath our walls, we shall let them pass," he finally said.

"And why wouldn't they?"

"Because they are cowards. They will not fight in the open unless they have overwhelming odds."

"That strikes me as common sense," I said.

"Then you know nothing of honor," said von Sievers.

"Honor aside, I will take them your proposal," I said.

Admittedly, I knew little of honor, or any of the other abstractions for which these Indigos were willing to give their lives, or take other's lives. At least the Italians fought over love, or better, wine, which is what they did when I returned with the German offer. Beatrice argued to accept, Aeneas to reject. The wine flowed and the band came apart under bitter ridicule of each other's ancestry, much like the fights in Paradise but for the choking and biting. In the meantime we ran out of wine and the argument was settled. After fighting each other bitterly, they paired off to grind their mouths and hips against each other in violent love-making, then fell asleep near the fire entwined in each other's arms, Aeneas and Beatrice included. In the late morning we drank from those ground-up, bitter, black beans, called coffee, and mounted up wordlessly to march under the horrible walls of Munchen.

XLII

I now had my own horse and, if not capable of convincing the beast that I was its master, I was getting better and better at, as Beatrice put it, sitting as fast as it could run. It is actually quite exhilarating, for they are huge creatures born for grazing or running and at top speed leave the ground for meters, their great legs pausing in flight and then catching themselves again in stride. I suppose this is not the time to go off on that, but I must remind you that this book writing thing is yet rather new to me.

Not long after mid-day we came to the edge of the city, its storminess blacking out the sky above it in smoke, the Valkyrie moaning in the air above us beneath their lucid wings. The Italians had painted themselves and their horses in white, green, and red. They said not a word.

As we approached the dark walls a thousand Germans lined the top with strange arrow slinging devices and hollow tubes which they pointed in the air to release bangs and smoke.

"*Machinas*," Beatrice said to me.

The city literally stunk and belched, the Germans shouting insults from its protecting walls as the naked Italians came forward in a line. Then as we came under the center of the wall, Aeneus first, then all the others, turned their horses to face the gates and the Germans above us.

"Just walk forward," I said to him. "Don't taunt them."

"We are not afraid of them," he said

Each Italian raised a lance into the air. The Germans above quieted. They lowered their weapons and pointed them downward upon us. In any book I have read since, this was certainly the moment for a blunder, an insult, a misconstrued gesture which might begin our slaughter and my ensuing, breathless escape as the Germans piled from their gates and hurled their armored selves upon us from their horses and from their walls. But in fact, nothing happened. Nothing at all.

The Italians lowered their lances and marched beneath the walls of Munchen and the Germans, true to von Sievers word, let them pass. If we rode with any desperation toward the plains of Firenzi it was due to our empty wine sacks, as the Young Italians pushed their animals mercilessly from day to night, through the night and toward the dawn, to home and wine.

Finally, we came upon a long, flat expanse that sloped upward and then descended again into a dry, open plain. In the distance, a patch of green took shape, indicating an oasis which, as we approached, showed itself to be a steep valley, almost a canyon, through which a small river flowed; though its origin seemed a mystery, the river itself extended south and west into flatland and along it I could make out the patchwork of crops, an unusual sight, for so little of home was now flat and dry and what little gardening occurred there came in the form of small terraces on the outside of stacked flats; here, the sight of wheat and corn sweeping from the river banks and into the dry plain, was breathtaking. I gazed intently for the buildings of Firenzi, but as of yet saw little besides the foliage of the oasis. Beside me, Beatrice and the others pulled up their steeds and crossed their fists over their chests. Aeneas sent Dante ahead.

"So they can prepare for our entry," Beatrice told me.

"Will there be singing and celebration?" I asked. "Poetry?"

"Don't be cynical, Marl," she said. "The more poetry, the longer your life."

"I'd regard myself lucky in any case," I said.

"You're cynical and lucky. I see Arab ships," she said.

"You can see that far?"

"Their poem lasts a thousand nights."

"Is it a good story?"

"It's a long story. I would not be an Arab woman. Our horses have more freedom than their women," she said.

"Where do they live?"

"They're nomadic traders. They pay us not to prey on them. Maybe one of them will want to buy you."

"I have too much respect for the Young Italians to believe them capable of selling me," I said.

"You can stick your respect up your ass, Marl," Beatrice said.

Dante returned and we began our advance into Firenzi. I expected a gardened city, cobbled streets, brick mansions and multi-storied buildings with balconies, domed churches; the fabled, historic Firenzi of Home to which even the Nutian traveled as tourists, but on the edges of the small river there was only the sprawl of conical tents, horses tied at the doorways, dogs and children running about in the dust. A small crowd greeted us as we entered and a woman stepped forward, Aeneas' mother, Beatrice told me, Circe. She was very tall, dark skinned, with thick, black hair falling over her shoulders and around her robes.

"What have you brought us?" she said.

"The pride of successful battle," Aeneas said to his mother.

"English tea?" said Circe.

"We wreaked havoc across the plains," said Aeneas. "The Germans trembled above us. The Austrians yet weep in their ruins."

"That was trembling," I said to Beatrice. "What the Germans did."

"That's called vandalism," said the woman. "Worthless teenagers," she said.

"We have a valuable prisoner," said Dante. He prodded my horse to the front.

"*Buena dia, Senora,*" I said. "*Tu es multi bella.*"

"A short man with a bad accent?" said Circe.

"He's Nutian," said Aeneas.

"Nutian are lizards," said Circe.

"Nutian are amphibians," I said.

"Fish eaters. You're a long way from fish."

"Maybe not," I said.

"That's why he's come," said Beatrice.

"Because you're an amphibian?" said Circe.

"No," I said. "An ambassador."

"A non-amphibian ambassador."

"Our prisoner," spoke up Beatrice.

"He speaks German," said Dante. "We caught him among the Austrians."

"I was in the middle of the desert. There wasn't an Austrian in sight."

"Then to whom were you speaking German?" Circe said.

"To fish!" said Dante.

"In the desert?" said Circe.

"To whales," said Aeneas.

"Oh yes, the desert whales," said Circe.

"There are desert whales?" I asked.

"If you eat enough peyote," she said.

"On Europa," laughed Beatrice. "Whales on Europa."

"Oh, the fish freighter fellow," said Circe.

"The fish freighter fellow?" I said.

"Let's kill him right away," said Circe.

"Not until he tells the German fish story," said Dante. "It's hilarious."

"Is it quick?" said Circe.

"It takes a very, very long time," I said.

"It does?" said Dante.

Beatrice laughed more.

"Shall we eat him?" Circe said. "Will he make us funny?"

"Eat?" I said.

"He negotiated safe passage for us beneath the gates of Munich," said Beatrice to Circe.

"Thank you," I said to Beatrice.

"Then his flesh will make us brave, too," Circe said.

"Not brave," said Beatrice.

"Not brave?" I said.

"I'm trying to help you," she said to me.

"Did you promise him anything?" said Circe.

"A quick death," Aeneas said. "If he insults us in Italian."

"You will find no fish speaking Italian here," Circe said to me.

"I'm not looking for them."

"You prefer your fish to speak German."

"I have no preference for what fish speak," I said. "I mean whales."

"Europa must be a horrible place," said Circe, almost wearily. "Frozen, German."

"Like Munich," said Beatrice.

"Do the fish drink beer as well?" Circe said.

"I never thought to ask that!" said Dante.

"Do you think we stole a freighter to teach fish Italian?" Circe said.

"Would there be another reason?" I asked her.

"This is growing increasingly absurd," said Circe, "is it not? What kind of ambassador would speak such nonsense?"

"Let's kill him!" Aeneas said.

"If he cannot speak plainly," Circe said.

Admittedly, the situation had become quite absurd, so much so that I contemplated that was exactly Circe's strategy. And the longer I spent on Mars, the more unlikely it seemed that anyone there was capable of anything besides nonsense and the stories that seemed to organize the nonsense.

"Are you in charge?" I asked Circe..

"We do not do *in charge*," said Circe.

"May we start over?" I said.

Circe turned to the small crowd behind her. "Let's just kill him," she said and there were shouts of "yes," and "that's good."

"Are those Arabs?" I said, pointing beyond the river to the wind ships. "Beatrice promised me their story."

There was a loud groan in front of me and behind.

"No!" said Aeneas. "Beatrice!"

"I did," said Beatrice.

Of course, she hadn't promised me, but she had become my tentative ally.

Then from behind the tents came a huge, sprawling fury of fur, a small hill of furry flurry. Elronhubbard floated furrily toward us and stopped at the edge of the encounter, a swirling of petting motion. "We—we—we," said the Elronhubbard. Even from a distance she smelled like baked hair. I listened closely for L's voice, but I could distinguish little from chorus. "Marl," they purred. "You don't smell so good, Marl."

The Italians, young and old alike, were greatly dismayed by the Pet's recognizing me.

"We can still torture him," grumbled Aeneas.

"Unlikely," said Beatrice.

In the meantime, the Arabs had arrived, surrounding us with their little windfull ships, some of them as small as Austrian snowboards; lifted by hooded sails, they skipped across the sand in flying leaps as their riders let out wild yips and howls. From among them emerged a slender man, dark skinned, who held his mouth and brow in a perpetual sneer, as if on the verge of both laughter and spitting. When he removed his hood he revealed a head of thick, black, flowing hair.

"Ali Kurtz Akbar," he said to me, bowing, speaking in Homan.

"Marl," I said. "You are Kurtz?"

"We are all Kurtz," said Ali. "As you are all Nutian."

"We are all Nutian," I said.

"We are all Kurtz," said Ali.

Well, that had gone as far as it could go, and I expected that could be forever.

"Stay with us," Ali said. "If the Roamin will be kind enough."

"I wish to go to Venezia," I said.

"Surely there is time for a good story," said Ali.

"A thousand nights," said Aeneas. He grimaced. "More than a year."

On home, of course, almost three.

"And more," said Ali, bowing to Circe.

Elronhubbard petted herself forward. "But who will tell it Kurtz-Ali?" said the Pet in her chorus. "Who?"

Ali's head rolled and his eyes swam in such a way as to present both hilarity and disdain. "Come, Marl," he said.

I dismounted. "Thank you," I said to Beatrice.

"You may be sorry," she said.

"To be saved from torture?"

"The Arabs have too many homes," she said.

"It seems they have none at all," I said.

"That is too many," said Beatrice.

But I was not sad to leave the Italians, young and old, for the cool and cozy confines of Ali Kurtz Akbar's tent; its walls draped in layers of colorful cloth and its floor covered with pillows. If the women there were not, as Beatrice warned, treated worse than Italian horses, they were abundantly at Akbar's service and brought us plates of desert figs and dates, platters of olives and flat bread with sharp, fresh cheeses, pots of stew made from animal flesh, and clear, cool water. I hadn't eaten so well since my first night on Gift Moon.

We did not take food from the service, but needed only to glance in the direction of something before it was delivered to our plates in abundance. Following Akbar, I ate with my bare right hand, even the stew, which I scooped with bread. We ate silently, Akbar's concentration on his food only broken occasionally when he lifted his head for a moment and offered a sneer. After the main course we were brought a delicate, if crumbly pastry, tasting a little like sweet, pressed dust, and a hot, black drink, coffee, similar to what the Italians drank at breakfast. Akbar finished, had everything cleared. He burped loudly and then seemed to chuckle with his whole body without showing any emotion on his face.

"You know the Pet," he said.

"Some of her, anyway," I said.

"And you don't like the creature."

"That is irrelevant, really," I said.

He nodded and waved his hand in front of his face as if chasing away an insect. "Yes, ambassador," he said.

"Thank you," I said to him. "You allowed me to survive. And contribute."

"Not really," he said, almost to himself. "If you do not find someone to tell you the tale, then I must return you to the Italians at dawn."

"How hard can that be?" I said.

"Among the Italians, not hard. But among us there must be a concubine."

"If I must," I said.

"And there are none here untaken," said Akbar. "The thousand stories were told because a great king caught his wife in an act of infidelity. After executing her, he slept only with virgins and had them slain in the morning."

"Deadly logic," I said.

"Well said, Ambassador Marl," said Akbar. "Shahrakurtz, the daughter of the king's closest advisor, taking pity on the women of her land, volunteered to sleep with the king and each night told him a story so fascinating that he fell asleep waiting for the end. But each tale opened up into another and another until a thousand were told."

"The day is saved," I said.

"More than a day," said Akbar.

"Kurtz doesn't die."

"Shahrakurtz does not die. Kurtz is another story. He is the father of us all."

"And dead, I assume."

"Death is a relative term," said Ali Kurtz Akbar.

"Why is the Pet, Elronhubbard, here?" I asked.

"It seemed to expect you," he said.

"I was expected here?"

"Yes."

"Do you trust her?" I said.

"The Pet?" said Akbar. "Trust is irrelevant."

A woman brought in a pipe in the shape of the dragon I'd seen repeatedly engraved on artifacts.

"I've seen this pipe design before," I said.

Akbar barely raised a brow.

"On the Gift Moon," I said.

"The Fish Moon," said the Arab.

We smoked, and it was the same sense-heightening drug I'd shared with the pirate, the Queen of Hearts, on Gift Moon. I said this to Akbar.

"And the Germans speak the same language as the fish," he said.

"They aren't fish," I said. "Do you know of the ghosts there?"

He withheld a sneer. "There are ghosts everywhere," he said.

"The Pet there was named Elmoleonard and I thought, well, I thought at first she, she sympathized against the Nutian," I said. "But later, when the carnivore whales attacked the fishing fleet, they killed the Pets along with the baleen workers. That's when I met the German speaking Orcas that everyone on Mars finds so fascinating."

"It's amusing," said Akbar. "But I don't follow."

I took some time to back track and explain. Then I said, "The Orcas are revolutionaries. Do you know the word?"

"They fight," Akbar said. "Here everyone fights everyone else. In Newamerica there are not even tribes. Individuals simply war on each other."

"But if the Indigos united, as the Orcas, dolphins, and sperm whales have done on Mars, you might stop the Nutian aqua-forming."

He did not, for lack of a better phrase, rise to the bait.

"Fish workers of the moon unite!" laughed Akbar. "We shall be fighting here long after the aqua-forming," he said.

"They are not fish."

"No," he said, "the fish are on your missing freighter." He waited; smoked more. "Why would the ambassador imply a war against the Nutian?"

"I am increasingly interested in why there has never been one."

"There is no bio-technology on Mars," he said.

"The Germans have machines," I said.

He might have snorted out his nose had he been given to anything but the intimation of the gestures and expressions of disdain. "They make smoke and toys. They cannot fly between planets."

"The Valkerie fly."

"They merely glide. The Germans fuss behind their walls and tremble in their armor. If it were not for we Arabs, nothing would come in or out of their cities. They couldn't hijack a camel, let alone a fish freighter."

"Then who did?" I said. "Kurtz?"

He offered me the pipe and I took it. "All things are possible, Ambassador Marl. Given that truth, is it not stunning how little really occurs and how miraculous is the pittance?"

"Can you take me to Venizia?" I said to Akbar.

"I am fascinated, Marl, by your refusal to comprehend your imminent torture and death," he said.

"Whether possible, inevitable, or impossible, it is irrelevant."

Akbar rose then, like a man floating within his robes. "May you have the pleasure of my palace until dawn, Ambassador," he said.

I sat in meditation, watching the shadows of torchlight dance against the moving walls. My journey here on Mars had been much like the Indigos themselves, a trail of bickering rumors and unconnected malice, bias and evasiveness, everything falling apart and no one willing or able to hold it together, even in the face of the destruction of half their planet, an act that would push the violent Indigos on top of each other into even more flagrant atrocities, more intense hatreds, more constant war. It was, as Akbar might say, the miraculous pittance. If the remnants of our species on Home were not isolated into the Wild Zones and separated by seas, they would likely be at each other's throats. Except for these stories. If they but shared one story among them, then there might be some hope. Yet there were a hundred thousand stories here, all of them about one being, and I could not decide between truth and charade, and where the reality in front of their faces ended and the unreality of their stories began, or was it the other way around? And if the story teller were Kurtz, or Kurtz the story told. It became, for me, a question of where to draw my circles, if the final one was the wordless empathy and quiet freedom of the Nutian, or if, in fact, that philosophy were yet the most recent conquering, and Kurtz now rose up beneath it like a thorn under its skin.

It does not take much thinking like that to bring the dawn. I saw the light creep at the tent walls, the torchlight extinguish, heard the voices outside mumbling low, repetitious chants, and then the regretful concern for my return to the tortuous Italians. The tent flap opened. And in stepped L. She moved to me, placed a hand on my cheek, another on my organ and brought me up, and in her soft down sat upon me face to face, her eyes like two dark nights. "In the name of Kurtz, the merciful, the compassionate," she whispered. "Praise be to the master of the Universe. May the lessons of these people be the lessons to the people of our time, so that we may see the things that befell others besides ourselves, and we will honor and consider carefully the words and adventures of past races. Glory to the preserver of the tales of the first dwellers. Take what is in them of wonder and instruction."

"L," I said.

"Sshh," said L. "Once there was a king of all kings who had two sons," she said. It was a long story and it took a long time.

XLIII

For more than a Martian year this is how we spent our nights and, as well, some of our days, though unlike Shahrakurtz, who held King Shahryar on the cusp of his desire, L told me the tales while locked in the embrace of passion. And if I made love to her a thousand times and one, never was there a story less interesting than another, and never was there once when I did not mark my life by the rhythms of our ecstasy and not think while inside her, while wrapped in the writhing of her softness, that each time was the best.

In the those moments between, in our quiet exhaustion, we lay beneath the breathing walls of the tent, tracing the sun's path, noting the faint translucence of the flying moons, listening to the sounds of a planet growing moist after a billion years of drought; the wind growing softer and more thick, the shadows heavier, the ground sucking breath, the sighing of the sky beyond. Between times, times ever so few, we lived on dates and cheese, water and flat bread left at the door along with a gift from Akbar, leafs of paper and what I have come to know as ink and pen, upon which, in the barren moments between bouts of love, I wrote much of what you have read.

Then, at some uncountable dawn, L upon me in the throws of dissipation, she held my face between her hands and related the escape of the lovers, Jasmine and Almond, under the wings of Destiny, and the inimitable marriage of Shahrakurtz and King Shahryar, who lived year after year in all delight, knowing days each more admirable than the last and nights whiter than days, until they were visited by the Separator of friends, the Destroyer, the Builder of tombs, the Inexorable, the Inevitable.

When Ali Kurtz Akbar came with his wind ship to take me to Venizia, I was more Indigo than they were themselves, and wanted more for them: the transformation of a world, but not from sand to water, but from quiet awareness to madness and depth, to an avarice so unquenchable that placidity lived only on the edges between the suckling rage.

I clung to L as Akbar's schooner skirted the desert toward the basin once known as the Hellas, but which now held the lake city Venizia where the inhabitants moved about from home to home, to theater and shop, on frail boats between frail palaces so shimmering and pale it was as if they were mere reflections of the lake itself, mirrors of mirrors, reflections of mirages. "Look," I said to L as we flew down toward the magical city where the Kurtz fell in love and died. "There! A new sea!" A glistening sea rising from the sand, big enough for a dozen fish freighters and a million-billion fish, so glorious as to be unbelievable. "Unbelievable," I whispered to L.

"Only believable, Marl," she said. "A city written on the desert."

"And real!" I said. "It is more real than you and me."

"Maybe more than you and me," said L, "but only that real."

And indeed as we approached the lake, the buildings of the city began to disappear one by one, fading into the reflection; the boats sailing from us to the edge of the horizon, never to return; the people who waved from the balconies fell into the disappearing lake, which as we drew near turned into shining sand. There, finally, on the verge of the Hellas, we stopped at the edge of a stinking pond where a young lad sat; he wore a striped linen suit with a red breast knot and his eyes stared out, fixed upon the reflection of our sail as it danced in the light over the green surface.

"Tadzio," I said.

He stood and stepped into the shallow water, which at its deepest did not wet his knees, and waded idly. No Kurtz. No lake. No city of dreams. Just a boy standing in a pond.

He turned to me. "That is all there ever is," he said.

It was then and there that I wished it all had ended and I had returned to Home with L in my embrace, my mission a failure, yet with a found, quiet, embryonic life near a soft, blue shore, the water lapping upon the edges of my consciousness, my nights spent rocking in the lock of love and my days forgetting everything I had learned here on Mars, a planet of words and myth.

The boy, Tadzio, once more paused to look upon the reflection of our sail which now danced at his knees, and as if by sudden recollection or impulse, turned from the waist up, an exquisite movement, one hand resting on his hip, and looked over his shoulder to us at the shore.

"The Valles Marineris," he said. "The Marine Valley. You will find Kurtz there."

"The Valles," I said quietly, "is half way around the world."

"Then you are half way there," said L.

"Had I started out from Olympus and gone east instead of west I'd have been there three years ago."

L stroked me with her body, her hand petting my cheek. "You would have been somewhere very different," she said.

I looked back toward the boy, but now there seemed to be a large expanse of water between us.

"Don't watch him," L said. "Or when he disappears, you will die."

"Nonsense."

"Marl," said L, and tuned my cheek to face her. When I pulled away from her to gaze at the boy again he'd disappeared in a mirage of mist.

XLIV

It takes years to master a wind ship. Instead, Akbar gave us four camels, animals which seemed not to have changed much since their days on Home, but for growing slightly wider and lower to the ground, so that when you were upon them it was like floating in the desert on a furry boat. Though slower then horses, they were steadier and calmer, and much less often did you need to fill them with water. To watch them walk or run, you might swear they moved impossibly, always on the verge of tipping over or falling down, their legs bouncing and wobbling, yet as a rider on their backs you felt no movement at all, and if it were not for the thin wind against your face you might not know you were moving. You could hold a shallow bowl of water in your palm and not spill a drop, or, as I did with L, ride double, if you could call us, in those moments, two.

"Is this somewhat like being in a Pet?" I asked L.

"No," she said.

Akbar gave us a sack of medallions engraved with his name, though like the empty bird cage in Aschenbach's home, the letters took the shape of the mythical beast, the dragon. If we ever needed anything during our journey, or were threatened, we needed only to offer our host or enemy one of Akbar's dragons. If they returned the coin to Akbar when he passed through, he would know that they had helped us and repay them tenfold. If someone were found with more than one of the medallions in their possession, Akbar would know that they had been stolen and Ali Kurtz Akbar would have the culprit slain.

By the time I'd reached the Hellas I had, in fact, already traveled a good two-thirds of Mars. Now we traveled along the northern rim of this great crater, feted by Arab shepherds along the way. For the first time I saw some people carrying small booklets, like the one I saw on the floor of Aschenbach's villa, like the one I now carried with my own writing, stuffed between my aqua-leathers and my chest.

"Are those books?" I asked L.

"Book," L said.

"They are the same?"

"They are all different parts of the *Koran*. A God book. There are others."

"About a big, invisible cause," I said.

"All causality is invisible, Marl," said L.

"I assume you read that somewhere."

"Yes," she said. "Members of a tribe group who can read commit a section to memory, then teach parts to others. Everyone has a part they can recite."

As the Young Italians did around their campfires. And the Germans in their tents. Apparently the reading thing was hard to learn, the writing even harder.

"Who wrote it for them?"

"Kurtz, of course," she said.

"And how do some of them learn to read?"

"From subversives," said L. "Writing teachers."

"Like you," I said. "Is Kurtz God?" I asked her.

"Don't be ridiculous," L said.

"Then why are all the stories about Kurtz? Why not one story?"

"Then what would there be to fight about?" said L.

If on Home there was now one, peaceful, silent way to live, on Mars there were a thousand violent ways. We left the plains of Arabia; traversed a world and saw the tribes of Mars: African peoples who lived beneath the dunes in burrowed cities; Scandinavians who lived in domes of ice; a tribe of Brazilians inhabited the bodies of giant snakes; a race of Chinese lived on the backs of Condors that never touched the ground; there were cliff-dwelling Australians; Laotians who hung in caves like bats. Each had their stories. Each hated the other.

At the end of a hundred days we skirted the southern edge of the Valles Marineris and traveled westward along the northern border of the crater-pocked Newamerica. From every crater a structure rose like a needle and beyond the craters, primitive stone fences abutting other fences, inside each fence, the same animals and crops as their neighbor. Often enough, small pitched battles raged between families; they tore at each other with knives and swords and arrows and rocks; they tore down each other's fences and tried to expand their own. Here I saw my first signs, large flat placards which were hung on the edge of everyone's fences. They said: **PRIVATE PROPERTY** and **NO TRESSPASSING!** L said that these were the only words the Newamericans ever learned.

XLV

At the mouth of the Valles Marineris I saw the first real body of water, a lake of considerable width, at least two kilometers, and inestimable length. It sat remarkably blue and pristine against the red sand. Near the mouth of the Valles, a thick patch of green emerged, which we found to be hillsides of scrub bushes, the same as you saw now in desert oasis or on the sides of mountains where snow accumulated. There, amid the scrub and sage, was a small dock with several boats. Aboard one, with a single mast and sail, some black men and women unloaded fish to the shore. The creatures in their net were small, not the huge, ocean fish I'd seen on Gift Moon, and the water of the lake was fresh, not salt.

A man stood on the dock, dressed as did most Indigos, in layers of robes which could be added or subtracted depending on the weather of the hour or day, with a hood which could be lifted to protect the face from blowing sand. Even over her fur, L wore a light robe and hood like this, though I still wore my leathers and goggles, which worked fine enough and, I thought, left no doubt that I was the Nutian ambassador. L spoke to the dock man, Ifit, in a language I didn't know, though by the time we had given him his Akbar Dragon and procured a bark skiff with two sailors, I'd begun to understand the basics well enough. The boat was narrow on both ends and wide at the center where it accommodated a hut. It had fishing nets and small harpoons, lines and hooks which I came to learn were also used for catching fish, a small stove for cooking and warmth. It was propelled by long poles, stuck into the water and pushed off the bottom of the river, where we would be traveling against the current, though there were oars, as well, for when the water was deeper and the current less forceful.

Our sailors, Goha, the shorter of the two, with skin almost brown, and Hacob, a tall man with pepper hair and black-blue shining skin, at first took L for some kind of ape and were stunned when she spoke to them. As well, they wondered if I weren't some kind of creature from another lake.

"What other lake?" I said.

"A very strange lake," laughed Goha.

"And she is from a strange jungle," said Hacob, pointing at L.

"That's right," said L.

"She was of a Pet," I said.

"We know them," Hacob said. "They're gentle."

"But I've never seen one taken apart!" Goha laughed. I learned that he liked to laugh.

"And I am from Home," I pointed to the sky. Then I pulled back my leathers to expose the skin of my forearm. "I am not Nutian, but a Homan who goes to the dry planets for them."

"Then you might not be long for this place!" Goha said.

Though things did not go as well when I explained that we were not there for a fishing trip, but to travel the length of the Valles. They rubbed their chins and stared off.

"I am here to see the Kurtz," I said. "How far down have you been?" I asked.

"Half," said Goha.

"But surely people go there."

"Not my people," he said.

"I have been there with the old man," said Hacob. He pointed to the dock. "We took a Pet. And Nutian."

"Nutian have their own ships," I said.

"Then where is your ship?" said Hacob.

"That's a long story."

"Is Kurtz in it?" asked Goha.

I hesitated.

"Yes, in fact he is," said L.

"But I can't tell it now," I said.

"We might have a lot of time soon," he laughed.

"The creatures in the Valles River are not kind to Nutian ships," said Hacob.

"They eat them," said L.

"Yes," said Hacob. "So the old man and I have taken them in. When I was the apprentice. It's apparent now, isn't it? Why I am here with you."

"And out?" I said.

"They didn't come out."

"There are Nutian already in there?" I said to L.

"In one way or another," L said.

"What way and what other?"

L took two dragons from the bag and gave one to each of our sailors.

"This is a good day," laughed Goha. "I woke up a fisherman and now I have a career."

Before nightfall we unloaded our gear from the camels and onto the boat. I gave two of the camels to Ifit and told him to keep one each for Hacob and Goha upon their return. If need be, I'd buy them back. We camped on the shore of the lake, at the river mouth, and I found my soft privacy with L under the streaking moons.

"Have you led me around the planet like a fool?" I asked her.

"A fool is taken to the truth right away so he can deny it right away," said L from my lap. "I wouldn't deny you any information that would bring you harm, Marl."

"Is the freighter down there?"

"I don't know."

"Is Kurtz?"

"I think so."

"So you've denied me information."

"I'm a teacher, Marl, not a spy."

By that I was supposed to understand that there were things I was ready to learn and things I was not ready to learn.

"You are a spy," I said.

"Of course I am," said L.

XLVI

In the morning we began our journey into the river of darkness, Hacob and Goha pushing the boat along with their poles, though occasionally Hacob worked a hand rudder at the back of the boat. In a matter of days he'd shown each of us how to pole and row, as well as steer with the rudder, and Goha taught L and me how to drop and retrieve the fish net, and how to bait and hook the lines that we dragged as we trolled the river. At times there were different baits for different parts of the river, various grubs, bugs, and worms, though as we traveled deeper we began to bait the lines with the flesh of fish we'd already caught.

There, closer to the lake, the water was clear, even as it flowed between rocks, and sometimes we bathed in eddies or briefly swam beside the boat, all but for L who did not care much for water and used it sparingly to clean her fur. I became fond of watching her preen in the sun at the bow of the craft, methodically dipping her hand into the river, and then a steady self-petting with first the back of her fingers and then the her palm, from head to toe.

I went to her. "Teach me," I said.

"You don't have any fur."

"How to clean you," I said. I dipped my hand in the river and brought my fingers to her cheek, but she stopped me, holding my wrist.

"You are not a Pet, Marl."

"Neither are you, L," I said.

"And what are you? Nutian? Homan? *Human?*"

"What if I'm trying to be human?"

"Because humans love?" she asked. "Don't love me, Marl."

But what was I to take that to mean, here in this land of words where only words meant and as often as not were used to mean the opposite.

"We just fuck," I said. "Just clutch, paw, grab, embrace, nip, plunge."

"That's right," she said. "No little human kindnesses."

I looked to the red cliffs above us, and to the shore where the vegetation had slowly become thicker, greener. At times I thought I saw movement behind the foliage, a rustle of leaves, a pair of eyes.

"Have I ruined everything, Marl?" said L.

And for a moment I thought she had, even until that night when she came upon me again and brought me to her, her softness in rage and flow, her voracious teeth upon my flesh, her breasts and thighs surrounding me with the pleasure of near suffocation.

"You see," she said to me, "I've only made it better."

XLVII

Until then we'd camped on shore, mooring the boat between rocks and making our fire on the open sand, but as the vegetation grew thicker we began to here the sounds of the night, the hoots and whistles of creatures and birds, a distant roar, a faint pounding. The river had grown deep and green and in places the four of us now used the oars. We now baited our lines not with the flesh of small fish, but with the small fish themselves, and the animal we caught that day was as long as my arm, black and fleshy, with eyes on the top of its head.

"We will sleep on the boat now," said Hacob. "The vegetation is too thick. There are predators."

"Better to be swallowed by a big fish!" laughed Goha. He nudged my arm. "Now it's time for your story!"

"Host first," said L.

"Gaa!" said Goha. "I hate when people know things!"

Over the next fortnight he told us the story of a young prince named Kurtz who played the lyre so beautifully that anyone of good heart who heard him fell under his gentle power, but those who harbored malice or greed had their jealousy exposed. Kurtz's uncle, who aspired to the throne and so feared Kurtz, plotted with Kurtz's mother and murdered the king. The treacherous pair framed the prince and banished him, then married and assumed the thrones.

While sent away, Kurtz joined a group of adventurous sailors and rounded the world slaying monsters, accumulating treasure, finally saving a kingdom under attack from men who used machines to do their fighting. There Kurtz fell in love with the princess Eurydice and they wed. Having saved one kingdom, together with the band of sailor-warriors Kurtz returned home where they defeated the army of the treacherous king and queen. King Kurtz and Queen Eurydice ruled with generosity and justice, and each night Kurtz played his lyre, bringing calm and peace to the just, rooting out the unjust.

But one day while Kurtz was hunting, the machine men returned and attacked his people, slaying many and taking the rest, including Eurydice, captive as slaves. Kurtz once again gathered his adventurers and set sail to find his enemies. He crossed a great sea and fought many battles until reaching the land of the machine men. In the ensuing battle, each of his great adventurers was killed from afar by weapons that did not even have to touch their victim to slay them. Kurtz fought on, receiving many wounds until finally coming upon the dying Eurydice, poisoned by her captors.

Distraught and enraged, Kurtz fled the battlefield for the kingdom of the dead and struck a bargain with the ruler of dead souls that he would stay and play his lyre there forever if he could only be reunited with Eurydice. Upon hearing Kurtz play, the ruler of the dead granted Kurtz' wish upon the condition that he never look upon his love or she would disappear into nothingness. Kurtz made the agreement and Eurydice came to him. Yet when she touched him, his longing to see her again was so great that he plucked out his own eyes so that he would never violate his promise. But his love was so deep that his eyes, laying bloody at his feet, yet gazed at Eurydice, whose hand slipped from his as she faded and fell into the nothingness beyond death. You can hear Kurtz's mournful lyre even now when you put your ear to the earth.

XLVIII

We'd traveled farther than Goha had ever been. The vegetation around us grew so thickly that the Martian sun was often hidden by a tunnel of vines and trees. Above us, animals skittered in the branches and in the brown water below, eyes peered out to watch our passing. We lived upon the boat now and never left its deck. The day after Goha finished his tale, the jungle surged around us with attention, and that night the distance no longer murmured, but was filled with the pounding of drums. At times, I was certain that we were followed from the shore by intelligent eyes, almost certain that I saw the movement of white, human forms slashing between the trees at the shoreline.

"The Whites," Hacob said. "They are the drummers."

"Do they want anything?" I said. "Are they just watching?"

"Maybe our lives," said Hacob. "I don't know."

"They don't always kill," said L.

"Sometimes just one is enough," Hacob said.

"You didn't say anything about them," I said.

"Some don't believe in them. Sometimes you don't see them at all," he said.

"So they want us to see them," I said.

"I assume," Hacob said.

"What do we do?"

"Mind our own business," Hacob said.

"Tell a very, very good story!" said Goha.

"They'll listen?"

"They are all around us now," said Hacob.

"*I'll* listen!" Goha said. "It will help me mind my own business."

That night, after we had eaten, we sat around the cook fire under the thunder of drums.

"They're closer now. The drums," said Hacob.

I took the leaves of paper from my pocket and lit my small stick light.

"What is that?" said Goha.

"Writing," said L.

"No, the light," said Goha.

"It's like a firefly," I said.

"I know of writing," Hacob said. "It tells stories, but it still needs a person."

I opened to the first page. The jungle dripped above us with its chattering, its shining eyes. From the foliage at the shore came a hooing, like the pushing in and out of breath, like a hundred beings breathing, the river hissing beneath us like an artery of a heart, Mars, hungry, violent, and alive, Mars unimaginable. There, I began to tell my story of Kurtz. "There has never been a good reason to be anywhere, let alone here," I read. "Yet here I am."

XLIX

We floated upon the black river, its black vegetation hung above us like lungs. The previous night, as I began my tale, the drums beat around us incessantly, into the dawn, into the lifting gray light beneath the canopy of trees, and now into the pale shifting light of day. The drums. The drums. The drums, and then, as we came around an elbow of the river, silence. Even the skittering in the trees above fell quiet and nothing stirred but the pish of water sliding against our bow.

As we came around the bend I saw the first of the Whites. He stepped from the jungle, as white as bone, but flesh, naked and white. Then another and another. They filed along the shore, white, the jungle at their backs, they stood absolutely still. A hundred. Two hundred. Three. As white as the white ghosts of the Ghost Moon. And then at once, their breath in unison, a giant, whistling lung, until I recognized that it was more then breathing.

"L" I said. "Do you recognize that?"

"The smell?" she said. "No."

"The whistling," I said. "The tune."

"They smell white," L said.

"It's frightening," said Goha from the stern.

"The work song of the dolphins," I said. "The ghosts."

"I don't think so," said L.

"It is!"

We passed a hundred more and a hundred more.

"These aren't ghosts," I said to Hacob.

"I'm afraid not," he said.

"Then what?"

"They are the Whites," he said. "This is theirs."

I swore, it was more than a whistle, but a tune, the same ghostly tune. But just as suddenly as it had begun, it stopped. The line of a thousand white figures stepped back into the jungle and forward came two muscular, giant beings, a woman and a man. The jungle resounded again with drumfire and the pair danced on the shore in inexplicable contortions; they screamed white, they danced white and blindly, they danced with all the violence a world could hold.

Goha yowled and hid his face.

"Your eyeballs would see them, even if you plucked them out," Hacob said to him.

"The King and Queen," said L.

"Of the Whites," whispered Hacob.

"Are they allies of Kurtz?"

"I have never seen Kurtz," Hacob said.

"You've never seen these either," I said. "What have you heard?"

"They are neither his enemies nor his friends."

"They're bad luck, though, Marl," L said. "If you see them, you die."

"You die anyway," I said.

The pair danced and danced as we passed. They pushed their groins forward and urinated at the boat. They screamed hellishly.

"She is right, it's a death sentence," said Hacob. "We will not finish the journey."

I went to the back of the boat and grabbed a pole. I pushed Goha to his feet. "Push!" I said. "Let's go!"

"It doesn't matter," Hacob said. "Leave him alone."

"Push!" I yelled.

Hacob walked to side of the boat and faced the dancers. He lowered his arms and turned his palms outward. A rain of darts fell upon him and he collapsed.

"In the hut!" yelled L. She dove for the center of the boat. "Get down!" But I saw a dart had entered her calf.

I pulled Goha from the stern to the floor of the hut, but already he'd taken darts in his chest and neck. I pulled them out. He tried to smile at me. "When next we meet, you will finish the story," he said. Then he died. The darts fell against the side and roof of the hut in sharp cascades of thuds and thaps, raining on us in fusillade; the boat swaying from their force until the hut teetered, then collapsed over us. Another round of darts fell upon us as we lay in the rubble of the shack. We lay silent. The deadly rain fell once more. Then again. And then stopped.

"Out of darts?" said L. She'd pulled the dart from her calf and tried to make a tourniquet by tearing strips from Goha's robe. In a little time the sounds of the jungle came back, though our boat listed and creaked, floundering broadside in the current. I bailed water, then wandered from the rubble to check Hacob. He was dead, too. The boat stunk of poison. I used our dead guides to balance our listing craft, then went to the back of the boat. Turning the rudder and poling forward, I managed to right us against the current and moved us another kilometer upstream before I anchored the boat and collapsed. By then, L had already begun to fever.

"Keep up the good work," she said to me.

"What do you need?"

"I'm dying."

"No," I said.

"Yes," L said.

L

That night I kept L cool with water from the river. I held her and rocked her.

"Leave me alone," she said.

Through the next day, as I poled the boat onward, her fever rose, and by night, anchored, she was frail and almost speechless. I took her hand.

"Like Eurydice," she said.

"Don't be ludicrous."

"What have you written?" L said.

"What can I do for you?"

"Have you related what happened?"

"Of course not."

"Write it down, Marl. Write me alive."

"While I watch you die?"

"Yes. Write me life."

And so I wrote what you read in front of you now, writing into the dawn. In the depth of the Valles Marineris, of Mars, deep in the jungle, the Whites, the deaths of Goha and Hacob, and finally, me, sitting beside L, watching death rattle in her throat, until her breath fell silent. She opened her eyes and looked at me.

"You don't smell so good," I said.

And then L died. I put my head against her breast. On the black river. In the black night. Thus it happened and thus I wrote it. I sat beside her and wept. I couldn't remember the last time I'd cried; some years ago; some many years ago, a century ago when I was a boy, no, yet a man, though young, at the death of my mother.

I looked at L and took up my pen. I wrote: But in the morning she awoke, very much alive. She sat up, preened. Took my head in her hands.

"Back from the dead?" I said.

"Power of the written word," said L.

"I should rewrite Goha and Hacob," I said.

"Don't push your luck," said L.

And there, just then, for that moment—didn't you feel it, too?—it seemed as if she were not dead at all.

LI

This is how I reached the Kurtz, on my crumbling boat of death. The people who received me silently emptied our bodies ashore, live and dead, and there on the sand we built pyres and burned them. A young man came to me with a shell of cool water. He had pale skin and full lips, long wavy hair, eyes of gray marble. He looked a little older, but I recognized him.

"Tadzio," I said.

"L was a hero," said Tadzio.

"Will Kurtz see me?" I asked.

I followed him through the jungle for a ways to the foot of a plunging waterfall. We walked along an edge behind the water, through a cavern, and out the other side where sat a hut. There was a gated archway made of bones twisted into the shape of two dragons, one on its chest, its tail curling skyward, the other sitting, its mouth reaching to the other's tail. They formed the entryway through a haphazard fence which looked, at first, as if it were made of thorn bush, but as I approached I saw that the dead vines surrounded a thicker, mud wall embedded with Nutian skulls, their teeth black, nostril and eye sockets gaping, the ambassadors of an empire that stretched beyond the solar system. And if I regarded this monstrosity with horror, then no more than the realization that the coming of the Nutian to Home, to Earth, was no return at all, and whatever the path of human depravity and where it had led, we were not, now, a saved species, but a conquered one.

I followed Tadzio through the horrible gate and into the hut. It was a house of old books, books stacked in columns and along the walls, books in piles and rows, a maze of books, a labyrinth.

"Where is Kurtz?" I said.

"This is the Kurtz," said the boy.

"And the freighter," I said.

He pointed to my chest, then touched it lightly where my book protruded. I took the writing out. He took the pages from me and pointed to the first page. "There it is," he said.

It was not time for that argument, if there was, in fact, any argument left.

"You have written the first new book," Tadzio said.

He took me to the back of the hut where a placard lay on the floor, framed in interlacing dragons. It said:

Lisa Zu
1999 – 2087

"A grave?" I said.

"She brought the books," said Tadzio.

"Five hundred years ago," I said. I tried to let it all come together, but this was Mars and here nothing came together. Here, one thing led to another, which led to another, which led to another, which led to nothing.

"Finish your book here," said the boy. "Leave it for us."

"Tadzio," I said, "in a decade this whole valley will be under water."

He looked at me with the same gaze that he offered from the stagnant pond in the mirage that was Venizia. "Maybe," he said. "Leave your book. Maybe everyone on Mars will come to tell its story and we will unite."

"How could that happen?" I said.

"How can anything happen?" said Tadzio.

I stayed a thousand days more and read a thousand books. Some were very much like the tales I'd heard on the surface of Mars, some were not; none had a character named Kurtz in them but for one, and it was a story that no one else told. Of my mission, and those I met here, I know nothing more than this, these words, this story. I have finished this book and now leave it. I imagine somewhere in the solar system, as you read this, that I am Kurtz. And whether there is great change or none, whether or not Mars, as so many other planets, has been buried in water, or revolution, whether or not our species has been subjugated or we have risen to the rule of our own nightmares; whether peace reigns or love rages, whether there is harmony or war, cast your words against the silence.

About the Author

CHUCK ROSENTHAL is the author of seven novels (including *The Heart of Mars*) and a memoir. He lives in Topanga Canyon, California.

Printed in the United States
67761LVS00006B/319-363

9 787774 581577